# CALL UP

# THE

# WATERS

# CALL UP

# THE

# WATERS

*stories*

# AMBER CARON

MILKWEED EDITIONS

All rights reserved. Except for brief quotations in critical articles or reviews, no part of this book may be reproduced in any manner without prior written permission from the publisher: Milkweed Editions, 1011 Washington Avenue South, Suite 300, Minneapolis, Minnesota 55415.
(800) 520-6455
milkweed.org

Published 2023 by Milkweed Editions
Printed in Canada
Cover design by Mary Austin Speaker
Cover photographs by Rawpixel and Bernard Gagnon Creative Commons Attribution-Share Alike License
Author photo by Andrew McAllister
23 24 25 26 27   5 4 3 2 1
*First Edition*

Library of Congress Cataloging-in-Publication Data

Names: Caron, Amber, author.
Title: Call up the waters : stories / Amber Caron.
Description: First edition. | Minneapolis, Minnesota : Milkweed Editions, 2023. | Summary: "A magnetic debut collection of stories about the daily lives of girls and women in rural America"-- Provided by publisher.
Identifiers: LCCN 2022049775 (print) | LCCN 2022049776 (ebook) | ISBN 9781639550449 (trade paperback) | ISBN 9781639550456 (ebook)
Subjects: LCGFT: Short stories.
Classification: LCC PS3603.A7674 L67 2023  (print) | LCC PS3603. A7674  (ebook) | DDC 813/.6--dc23/eng/20230104
LC record available at https://lccn.loc.gov/2022049775
LC ebook record available at https://lccn.loc.gov/2022049776

Milkweed Editions is committed to ecological stewardship. We strive to align our book production practices with this principle, and to reduce the impact of our operations in the environment. We are a member of the Green Press Initiative, a nonprofit coalition of publishers, manufacturers, and authors working to protect the world's endangered forests and conserve natural resources. *Call Up the Waters* was printed on acid-free 100% postconsumer-waste paper by Friesens Corporation.

For Seth

# CONTENTS

# CALL UP

# THE

# WATERS

# THE HANDLER

WHEN LESLIE ARRIVED in Jefferson, New Hampshire, Brent picked her up from the bus station wearing ripped jeans and a flannel shirt that had been cut off at the elbows. It was twenty-five degrees. It was January. It appeared he was sweating. He opened the passenger-side door, put his hand on her back, and helped her into the truck. Leslie guessed he was older than she was but younger than her father. She found it difficult to name a man's age.

"Moved here in ninety-five," he said. "Never got around to leaving." He sped up around the hairpin turns, pointing out every bend in the river, every mountain peak, every place there had ever been a car accident serious enough to kill. Each crash site was marked with a yellow ribbon and a bundle of fake sunflowers. He steered with his knees so he could light his cigarette, and Leslie forced herself not to grab the door handle.

He kept talking. Constellations. Moon cycles. The flood of '97. The blizzard of '99. The fire of '05. When they finally pulled up to the house, the dogs erupted, and Brent went quiet.

Siberians, Alaskan malamutes, Akitas, Russian wolfhounds, salukis, Saint Bernards, and mongrels—greyhounds mixed with Newfoundlands and a dash of

Belgian shepherd; Labradors mixed with coonhounds. Their names had been painted on the green wooden boxes they slept in: Mars, Frost, McGee, Bandit, Minnow, Tip, Empire, Stewpot, Pluto. Back of the property was the Scooby-Doo litter: Velma, Scooby, Shaggy, Daphne. Next to them, the pianists: Billy Joel, Elton John.

"That there is Ray Charles," Brent said, pointing to the glassy-eyed dog at the end of the line. "Was named Ray Charles before he went blind."

Leslie bent over to take the dog's muzzle in her hands. His nose twitched. He lifted a paw.

"Well, maybe you should start naming them after millionaires," Leslie said.

"I like it," he said. "A sense of humor. That will help you here."

Before she'd boarded the bus for New Hampshire, Leslie had left her boyfriend, Dennis, a voice mail: *I'm leaving you*, she said. *This time for the woods and fifty-seven dogs*. It sounded funnier when she'd rehearsed it in her head. She waited all night for him to call back and talk her out of it, and when he didn't, she got on the bus even though she no longer wanted to.

Brent bent down and lifted the dog's back leg. "First and foremost," he said, "your job is to take care of their paws." He brought the paw close to his face. "No paw, no dog."

He said it again, like a mantra, and taught Leslie how to check for ice balls between their toes; lacerations, abrasions, swelling, and cracks on the pads; abscesses and inflamed nail beds. "In three months, these paws need to get me from Anchorage to Nome," Brent said.

Fifty-seven dogs. Two hundred and twenty-eight paws. Leslie wanted to show it all to Dennis.

That first night she couldn't sleep through the country sounds. Wind in the trees. Dogs calling to a distant coyote howl. A train on the other side of the valley. When the sun came up, Leslie's eyes had already adjusted to the light.

She dressed and went outside. Brent was waiting on the front stoop of her cabin, halfway through a sentence she had to imagine the beginning of.

". . . dry food. A hunk of frozen beef. A ladle of chicken broth. Twice a day. While they eat, you scoop their shit into this bucket, and dump it over there, past that stand of pines." Brent pointed in a vague direction. There were pine trees everywhere. She followed him to the shed behind her cabin.

"And you'll want this, too." Brent pulled an ice pick from a hook. "The shit freezes overnight," he said. "You got to chip it into the bucket."

It took Leslie three and a half hours to finish morning chores. By the time she had rounded up the empty bowls, cleaned the yard, and checked all two hundred and twenty-eight paws, she had three blisters on her palm and a bloody shin where she'd clipped herself with the ice pick. One of the dogs had lunged for her ear, three dogs tried to hump her leg, and another mounted her back. At 10:00 a.m., her stomach was still empty, but the smell of blood from the raw beef made her want to retch. *Not funny anymore*, she thought.

Brent stepped out onto the porch of the big house, waved Leslie over, and disappeared back inside. She trudged across the snowy lawn and found him standing at the stove in the kitchen, a book in his hands, a line of jars on the counter. He pulled out a large pot from beneath the sink.

"We make our own salve," he said. "Too expensive to buy the other stuff. And it's got a bunch of crap in it, anyway. This is all you need." She looked at the recipe: Vaseline, Betadine, lanolin, glycerin, vitamin A, vitamin E. He went to the stove. "I'll help you with this first batch."

Leslie measured and poured according to the recipe. Brent talked and stirred and talked more. Behind her, Leslie heard footsteps coming down the hall. A girl appeared in her pajamas, her hair in a high ponytail, eyes wide set like Brent's.

"This is my daughter, Jill," he said. He put his arm around the girl as though they were posing for a picture. She shrugged him off. "This is Leslie," he said. The girl rolled her eyes and reached for the bananas on the counter. Leslie turned back to the stove and pretended not to be offended, and the girl dragged her feet down the hall.

"She's deaf," Brent said. "But that's not the reason she won't talk to you. She won't talk to you because she's thirteen. Also, she doesn't want you here." Brent moved the pot off the burner and grabbed a funnel from under the sink. "She wants to go to Alaska with me in March," he said. "To help with the dogs. When our handler quit last month, she thought she was a sure thing, since no one before you has ever taken this job in the middle of the winter."

"It's Monday," Leslie said. "Shouldn't she be in school?"

"Maybe," he said. "But she hates it. I don't push the issue."

"There are laws." Leslie filled one of the vials with salve, held it up to the light.

"You think anyone cares what a deaf girl and her musher dad are doing out here?"

"But she needs an education. I mean, even a high school education."

"You go to school?" he asked.

"Yeah. College. A few years of grad school."

He looked at her.

"And here we both are."

***

At the end of the first week, Leslie wrote Dennis a letter. She told him how the dogs ran for hours on the trails beyond the pines, and still they barked, cried, howled for more. She told him how she clipped nails, wrapped paws in booties, and massaged pads with the salve. She kept a small vial of it tucked close to her body so it would stay warm, and this made her feel like a doctor. At the end of the letter she wrote, *Come for a visit. I'll teach you.*

When a week passed without hearing from him, she wrote another letter. Each day she checked the mailbox at the end of the long dirt driveway.

***

All Leslie had eaten in her first two weeks was canned soup and granola bars, so when Brent invited her to the house for pork chops and mashed potatoes, she accepted.

Before they'd even finished loading their plates, Brent started talking. Race strategy, dog diets, harnesses. He'd raced the Iditarod twice, the Yukon Quest three times. He spoke slowly, story after story of his victories, of his run-ins with moose, of the time he rounded a corner on day thirteen of his first Iditarod and found an old boat frozen in the middle of the Yukon River. "It was a sign," he said. "I knew I'd win. I bootied every dog in under twenty seconds at every stop in that race. Shaved three hours off my time. That was the difference between first place and third."

Jill didn't take her eyes off her father's lips. Leslie watched them, too. They were chapped, a firm line down the middle like a cut that might open at any time. More gray than pink. When he chewed, the hairs of his moustache and beard touched.

"In her first race," he nodded at Jill, "she was disqualified when she took a wrong turn two miles in and raced the entire course backward."

Jill sat up straight now. She leaned in close to her father and watched him carefully.

"People tried to stop her, but she thought they were just cheering her on. She finished last. Two hours after everyone else. An hour after dark."

Jill swiped her hands through the air; Brent watched them. He laughed.

"She says blame Sass, her lead dog." He looked at his daughter. "User error, I'd say."

Jill's hands danced.

"My fault?" Brent said.

She went on. When Jill finally rested her hands on the table, Leslie noticed calluses and cuts, dirt lodged beneath her nails. Brent kept chewing. Jill pointed at him, then at Leslie.

Finally, he swallowed: "She says it's my fault for not letting her take my team."

Jill looked at Leslie, nodded once. Leslie smiled at her. Jill was unmoved. *We will not be friends*, that look said. She sliced her hands through the air again, and this time Brent put his fork down. When she finished, they stared at each other for a long time.

"I'm not telling her that," Brent said.

Jill stood up from the table, flipped her father off, walked through the dark house, and slammed a door.

———

Another week passed. More letters. She told Dennis that even when temperatures dropped below zero, the dogs had only hay to keep them warm. They slept with their tails over their noses. When they woke, they ran laps around their houses for something to do, making perfect little racetracks of packed snow. The swivel at the end of each of their chains clinked against the post, and the yard sounded like a chorus of finger tambourines. *Come for a visit*, she wrote. *Soon. Before I leave for Alaska.*

She was making her morning rounds when Brent returned from the mailbox with an envelope. The handwriting she would have known even without the name in the corner, and she took the letter inside. She ripped a neat strip from the edge of the envelope, turned it upside down, dumped the note onto her wooden table. It was written on the paper Dennis kept on the edge of his desk—the one with a picture of a pipe at the bottom. He hated the paper, but his mother had bought it for him when he turned thirty and gave up chewing tobacco for a pipe, and although Leslie had tried to get him to throw it away a dozen times, he said he felt too guilty. Instead, he used it for trivial matters. Grocery lists. To-do lists. Killing spiders.

She unfolded the paper. *Stop. Stop writing to me.*

That was it. Nothing more. Leslie tucked the note back inside the envelope, found a clean sheet of paper, and sat down with a pen.

Dear Dennis,

Stewpot has a fissure; Mars, a swollen ankle. Scooby's dewclaw is inflamed because I put his bootie on wrong. It started just as an irritation, but I ignored it, and now Scooby might be done for the season. Come visit next Saturday. It's lonely here.

Love, Leslie

They had been here before, the two of them. The first time she left him—the first warm day of spring two years ago, she remembered, the ground soaked with melted snow—he delivered a pile of soil to her backyard because she once said she wanted a garden. Each day after that, he left her packages of seeds—corn, squash, carrots, broccoli, red peppers, bell peppers—until finally, weeks later, on the day he brought her pumpkin seeds, she called him and said, *Fine, okay, stop with the seeds*. Six months later, when he ended it, it was her turn to lure him back, and she did it with ripe tomatoes, crookneck squash, overflowing bags of green beans, and bundles of basil. When he wouldn't open his door, she left the vegetables on his doorstep, adding to the rotting pile on her way to work, until one morning she showed up to find the doorstep clear of the rot and a note in its place: *Come in*, it said.

She got laid off from her job a week later and was pregnant just a month after that. He thought maybe they could do it. Maybe that child—and marriage, he said— was exactly what they needed. But the money, she insisted. He was only part-time at the warehouse. And besides, she already made the appointment. He said nothing more and showed up at the clinic where they held hands the way they had when they started dating. Leslie tried to ignore how sad he was in the weeks after, and she tried to hide her immediate relief, but once a week they yelled about it until she boarded the bus for New Hampshire. She hadn't expected to miss him.

She found an envelope and a stamp. She walked to the end of the driveway, the dogs calling after her, and shoved the letter in the mailbox.

———

Leslie was scrubbing the harness in the warming shed when Brent came in to stack the large green bags of food. The water in the bucket had cooled, and Leslie had to steel herself before she plunged each harness. The blisters on her hand were threatening to burst. Later she would poke each one with a needle and watch the skin sink back into itself.

"I was wondering if I could have Saturday off," Leslie said. She moved a harness from the wash bucket to the rinse bucket, where the water was slightly warmer.

Brent hauled two loads of food from the wheelbarrow to the corner before he spoke. "Going somewhere?"

"Someone's coming to visit," she said. "Just for the day. My fiancé." The word had slipped out, but Leslie found comfort in it. It was familiar and full of hope. She let it hang there. It had been true, almost.

Brent removed the ladder from the hooks at the far end of the shed and set it up in front of the stack he'd made, already taller than he was. He climbed, holding on with one hand, balancing a bag on his shoulder with the other. He reached the top, flung the bag onto the stack, and waited there for a moment to catch his breath. Leslie saw him look at her left hand. She pushed it deep into the water.

"Do your morning chores. Then you can have the rest of the day." He didn't look at her when he said it.

On Friday morning, while Jill watched her do the chores, Leslie couldn't help but feel the girl was collecting evidence of her insufficiency. After all the shit had been collected and each of the dogs fed, Jill went from doghouse to doghouse, peering into the doorways, talking to the dogs with her hands. She coaxed Sass out with treats and inspected her paws, pulled the skin back at the dog's cheek and scraped at her teeth. She rubbed the dog's chest, ran her hands down each leg, scanned the underside of the tail and inside the ears. Satisfied that Leslie hadn't ruined her lead dog, Jill tipped her head back and made her mouth into a tight circle, blowing puffs of hot air. Sass did the same, howling along to Jill's silent call.

---

That afternoon, Jill walked the perimeter of the property with a small white book. She stopped in front of a trunk, placed her hand against the bark, flipped pages, looked up, walked around the tree, flipped more pages. On and on, all afternoon. When Jill waved Leslie over, Leslie didn't move, certain Jill's gesture had not been for her. Jill waved again, this time with more urgency. Leslie went.

She wasn't sure what to do around the girl, where to put her hands.

Jill pointed to the tree. The bark was white and scarred with black lines. She turned to the section near the end of her tree guide. She put her finger on the bottom of the page. Quaking aspen. Scientific name: *tremuloides*.

Jill pointed to the woods and then back at the book. She swept her arms through the air and pointed again.

Leslie shook her head, shrugged her shoulders. Jill tried again, pointing from the book to the woods and to the book again. She stared hard at Leslie, waiting. Leslie still didn't understand. Jill put her hand into her coat and pulled out a pen and a notepad, flipped until she found a blank page, scribbled something, and handed the pad to Leslie: *Lots out there. A whole stand of them.*

"We used to have some," Leslie said, "behind the house where I grew up. My father called them weeds, cut them down, and—"

Leslie didn't finish the sentence because she could tell Jill couldn't understand her, couldn't read her lips the way she could read her father's. She took the pad and pen from Jill: *show me.*

The girl smiled, tucked her notepad in her coat. They walked together across the field, beyond the doghouses and the food shed. The morning wind had settled, but clouds were coming in from the south. Two crows were fighting in the pines. Somewhere a woodpecker was pounding on a tree trunk. Just before they entered the woods, Leslie heard a door slam, its echo holding for a moment in the valley before lifting into the gray sky. She turned. Jill followed Leslie's eyes. They watched Brent get into the truck holding an armful of yellow ribbons and fake sunflowers and disappear down the driveway.

Jill wrote: *Let's bring his team. Out to the aspen.*

Leslie shook her head. She pointed toward the driveway. Jill wrote again: *Changes all the ribbons at the crash sites! Gone all day.*

When Leslie pointed to the dogs, Jill wrote, *I'll help.*

When Leslie pointed to the sky, Jill wrote, *Tonight. No weather till tonight!*

Finally, Leslie took the pad and pen and wrote her own message: *I'll get fired.* Jill took the pen from her hand, scribbled something, and handed it back. *He won't fire you. Too close to race day.*

Leslie hesitated, looked back at the driveway, out to the woods, to Jill.

*He needs you,* Jill wrote, underlining her words twice.

Jill harnessed four dogs in the time it took Leslie to hitch one. With the towline anchored to the barn, all nine dogs lunged forward and leapt off the ground. Jill climbed onto the runners, and Leslie sat in the cargo bag, tucked between the dog treats, snow hook, and blankets. When Jill released the towline from the barn wall, the dogs sprinted forward, leaving the forty-eight others howling behind.

They headed west past her cabin and the warming shed, out beyond the aspen they had studied together, hugging the base of the mountains. The dogs kicked up snow as they ran, and Leslie shielded her eyes as best she could. But she wanted to watch them, the way the wheel dogs lunged forward and the swing dogs guided the team around the corners. They'd given up their howls for heavy panting, the occasional grunt. They worked. They did their job.

Once through the valley, they entered a stand of maples, oaks, and spruce. The bare limbs towered above them and the forest became a shadow of itself, dark despite the daylight, and the entire world—the snow, the trees, the bits of sky above, even the backs of the dogs—blurred together into a mass of gray. Jill guided the dogs and the sled through the trees, along a trail that had been traveled before but covered by recent snow. It wasn't until they were deep into the woods that Leslie saw the forest open up into hundreds of thin, white aspen.

Leslie felt the sled slow, and just before they came to a stop, Jill dropped the snow hook, the two steel prongs sinking deep into the ground. Stewpot and Mars, the workhorses in the wheel, looked back. Bandit plopped down in the fresh snow. Minnow peed.

Jill pulled her book out of her jacket and waved for Leslie to follow her. Beneath the trees, Jill opened the book and pushed it into Leslie's hand. She learned that a stand of aspen grew up to twenty acres of roots before sprouting an entire family of trunks, that every tree in a clone of aspen was genetically identical. She learned that birch bark peeled and blistered in the sun, but that aspen never lost its skin.

Jill took the book from Leslie, flipped through the pages, looking for something else. Leslie heard the dogs behind them getting restless. A sneeze, a whimper, Bandit and Mars pawing each other in play. But Inca's head was lowered, and the fur on her back raised. Leslie followed the dog's gaze.

Beyond the aspen, a patch of brown. Too big and dark to be a deer. Whatever it was disappeared behind the spruce trees, and rather than seeing the thing—bear? human?—Leslie could only trace the movement of the figure by the changing light through the trees.

The rest of the dogs, as though on Inca's cue, directed their attention to whatever was out there. Jill, still standing out by the aspen, absorbed in her book, hadn't noticed. Leslie watched until the figure emerged from behind the tall brush and into the edge of the opening.

Leslie tapped Jill on the shoulder, pointed. Jill dropped her book and ran for the team. The moose stared at the group for a long time, and the dogs pulled hard against their line. The snow hook didn't budge. When the dogs broke out in growls and barks, the moose took two steps forward. Jill swung her arms at the dogs in a silent command: *Stay.* The moose moved forward again, hooves disappearing into the fresh snow with each step. On the back of the sled, Jill pulled hard at the brake. All nine dogs lunged. The snow hook came loose. The dogs gave chase. The moose charged.

Jill tried to slow the team by tipping the sled. Leslie ran to help her, but it was already too late. The moose stomped its way through the dogs, tangling its legs in the gangline. A sharp collective yelp went up from the pack. The moose rose up and took aim at the sled. Its front legs crashed down on the runners, and Jill and Leslie fell to the ground. Leslie screamed at the dogs to stop, but nothing she said worked. Jill reached for the snow hook. When the moose stood up on its back legs again, an entire team of dogs biting at its backside, Jill swung the snow hook wildly, catching the loose skin under the animal's chin. The moose threw back its antlers, let out a guttural growl, and ran. It dragged the dogs and the sled behind it, until finally the towline caught on the trunk of an aspen, and the prongs ripped clean from the moose's chin. The animal slipped deeper into the woods, leaving a heavy trail of blood.

Leslie scanned her own body. She expected to be injured, but she wasn't. She hurried over to Jill, who pushed herself up onto her elbow and held her side. Leslie gently pushed her down so she lay flat on her back and ran for blankets in the sled. When Leslie returned, Jill pointed at the dogs.

Bandit—poor Bandit—gave Leslie a pitiful look as she unwrapped the tugline that had knotted around his neck. Minnow held up her back-left paw, and when Leslie looked at it, she saw a slice down the center pad. She found a bootie in the sled pocket, wiped the snow from between the dog's pads, and secured the strap around the leg.

She untangled the rest of the dogs, checked their paws and ears and ribs and legs. At the center of the pile of animals was Inca, still on the ground. Leslie knelt next to her, put her hand to the dog's chest—warm, but barely moving. She put her ear up to the dog's face and heard a long, low rattling. At the end of each breath, a groan.

By the time Leslie lifted Inca and Jill onto the front of the sled and got the pack reharnessed, the line of moose blood had frozen and turned black. Slowly, the team pulled their group back the way they came—through the aspen grove, along the base of the mountain—and Leslie watched Jill stroke Inca's ears.

———

Brent propped Jill up on her bed, pressed his hands to her shoulder blades, her stomach, her ribs.

"Three ribs, at least," Brent said. He didn't suggest a hospital, and when Jill twisted her fingers through the air and dropped her eyes, Brent watched but went outside without responding.

Jill reached for the pen and paper next to her bed. *He won't speak to me.*

Leslie took the notepad. *It wasn't your fault.*

*User error,* Jill wrote.

*I should have said no. I shouldn't have helped you.*

*I wanted him to fire you. I wanted to go.*

*You're thirteen.*

*He'll take you to Alaska.*

*I don't want to go.*

This was a lie. All she wanted was to go anywhere except across the field to the cabin she knew was dark and cold, where she would fall asleep alone on a cot in a sleeping bag that kept her alive but never warm.

Jill took the pad. *What did it sound like?*

*The moose?*

*No. Inca, dying.*

*Nothing,* Leslie wrote. *She died immediately.*

*Will you talk to him for me?*

*He'll get over it. They're just dogs.*

*You don't know him very well.*

Jill pointed to her pillow, and when Leslie tried to fix it for her, Jill shook her head vigorously back and forth. Leslie tried to shift it again, but Jill squinted, pushed herself up on her elbow, and fixed the pillow herself.

Leslie left her there and went out to check on Minnow. She pulled the vial from the breast pocket of her jacket, poured the salve into the palm of her hand, and massaged the dog's paw. Minnow she could touch without hurting.

———

Brent was in the warming shed when Leslie went in to make dinner for the dogs. It wasn't until she'd filled the water bucket in the sink that she saw Inca stretched across the ground, her legs straight and stiffened, perfectly still, her head propped on a blanket, as though she were asleep.

"She's sorry," Leslie said. "So am I."

"We'll have to get Sass ready. She'll take Inca's place." He rubbed the fur on Inca's neck.

"You have to talk to her. She feels terrible."

He ran his hands down Inca's legs, cupped her back paws, and tucked them into the black trash bag he'd placed at her feet. "We've got a month, which, for a dog like Sass, is plenty of time. She'll do fine." He tucked Inca's tail into the bag, then her front paws.

"I can get her harnessed up tomorrow," Leslie said.

"No," he said. "Do the morning chores. Then take the afternoon off like I promised." He pushed the bag up under her body until he got it to her neck. He ran his hand over Inca's face, gave each ear a scratch. "For your boyfriend."

"I'll help you bury her."

"Ground is frozen."

"What then?"

"The dump. They'll let me put her in the incinerator."

He pulled the bag over the dog's face, tied a knot, and hefted it into his arms. He walked to the door, the veins on his arms bulging beneath the black bag.

"Fiancé," she said.

Brent turned around. "What?"

"Not my boyfriend. My fiancé."

"Right."

Leslie watched him walk toward the truck and could see his lips moving. She knew he was whispering to Inca. The yard was silent, the rest of the dogs tucked in their houses, a few snouts resting at the opening of their green boxes, sniffing at the air behind the dead dog.

———

That night, weather came in. Snow, wind, ice, more snow. The line of spruce trees, their tops hunched over, looked like they were running from the wind. The oaks groaned;

two aspen snapped. The birds clutched branches and then disappeared on some invisible current. Even in the cabin, the wind pulled the heat from Leslie's neck, her cheeks, her eyes. Then it became all she could hear.

On Saturday, Leslie woke thinking of how, on the morning after they visited the clinic, Dennis had rolled over in bed, grabbed her hand, put it on his chest, and said it hurt right there. She'd pulled her hand away and left him in bed alone. But she felt it now, that darkness in her chest, and all she could think to do was climb out of her cot, layer herself against the cold, and do the morning chores. Food, shit, hay, paws.

Outside, the entire world glimmered white in the bright sun, but the snow, all eleven inches of it, with a thin layer of ice on top, looked razor edged and dangerous. She heard Brent in the barn, and when she went in, he was already working on Sass. He pushed an electric razor in and out of the pads of her paws, spread her toes, and trimmed around each nail. It was supposed to be Leslie's job. He lit a long taper candle and, moving the flame across the shaved pad, singed the hairs that were too small and too deep for the razor to reach. When the hairs sparked, Leslie expected Sass to yelp the way the dogs always did for her, but the dog, staring straight ahead at the barn wall, didn't move, didn't make a sound. Before long the barn was filled with the awful stink of charred hair. Leslie finished the morning chores and went back to her cabin.

Inside, she showered, put on her cleanest jeans and a real bra, not the sports bra she'd been wearing since she arrived, and dried her hair with the hair dryer she hadn't yet used. She left her hair down because Dennis liked it best that way, and she skipped lip gloss because he didn't like the way it felt when they kissed.

She sat in the rocking chair next to the window and watched Brent bootie up Sass. He straddled the dog, pushed the button of his watch, and began: he lifted one of the back paws, pushed the snow out of the pad, pulled the bootie on, wrapped the strap around the leg. Three more paws. Twenty-seven seconds. He did it again. Paw, push, pull, wrap. Twenty-five seconds. Again. Twenty-three. Twenty. He stopped when he hit nineteen—as Leslie knew he would—brought the dog back to her house, and walked across the yard to his own.

For the rest of the day, Leslie tried not to think of Jill inside, wrapped up in bed, holding her ribs. Or of Inca, her cold body in a black bag, or Brent, lifting the dog into a fire. Instead, she sat down to write another letter. She didn't ask Dennis to come for a visit because sometimes changing the subject worked better than begging. She only told him that Inca had died, knowing he would find that hard to ignore.

———

Hours later, in the dark, just before Leslie was about to give up and crawl into her sleeping bag, the dogs stirred. Like toddlers, Leslie thought. Screaming for attention, leaping onto their houses, trying to out-howl the others. Every sound—squirrel, rabbit, door—set them off.

Tonight she couldn't take it. She stood and reached for the door, but she heard someone climbing the steps to her cabin. It wasn't Brent—she knew his heavy gait. No, this was softer, less sure. A knock.

Leslie opened the door to find Jill hunched over, furious and in tears.

She pushed a piece of paper at Leslie. *He begged our last handler to go with him.* Jill snatched the paper back. *They're leaving next week! Three weeks early!*

When Leslie didn't respond, Jill wrote more. *He's taking Sass. She's mine!*

*You need rest.*

*I'm not going back in there.*

Leslie led Jill to her cot and covered her with the sleeping bag. Once settled, Jill wrote again. *You have to stay.*

Leslie turned the light off next to the bed. The bulb in the kitchen was barely strong enough to light the room.

Jill held out the paper once more. *You look pretty.*

———

After Brent left, Jill told Leslie that the two of them would race together the following season. Since she was still too frail to train the dogs, Jill trained Leslie instead. In the first week, she filled notebooks of instructions that Leslie studied each night: don't let them dip snow; don't let them play on the trail; be consistent; run McGee next to Legs, Basil next to Tarragon; give Pluto a good whack when he chases a rabbit; put Shaggy in the wheel, Velma in the lead. Make them work, that's what they want. In the second week, when Leslie confused the dogs with her commands, Jill pulled out a permanent marker and wrote *haw* on the top of Leslie's left mitten, *gee* on the top of her right. By the third week, Leslie was finally ready to run the full team.

Initially it was just in the morning, and she was always careful to stay within sight of the house. But then it was after lunch too, and then, if the dogs seemed as though they wanted more—they always wanted more—she'd take them out on Saturday mornings along the base of the mountains. By the fourth week, she was running them for hours, sometimes without even realizing it, never telling Jill when she was leaving or when she'd be back. It wasn't just the warming air that she liked, and how it felt on her face. It was the buds popping out on the trees. And the dogs, too. The way they listened to her. The way they turned left when she yelled "haw," the way they sprinted when she chanted "bring it on home."

It was after one of these long morning runs that she returned to find Jill hanging a large map of Alaska on a bare kitchen wall.

*Where were you?* It was already written on the notepad.

Leslie pointed out past the warming shed, past her cabin.

*For three hours?*

Leslie dug into her bag. She threw the dog treats on the floor, the headlamp, extra booties, the map, and the first aid kit, until she finally pulled out a book. It was wet from weeks of snow, and the pages curled up at the edges. The cover had faded, and the text was too blurry to read. But the tree on the front was still visible. Leslie had been looking for it on each of her runs that week.

Jill smiled, drew her fingers to her lips, then stretched them forward, opening her calloused palm.

"You're welcome," Leslie said.

They studied the map of Alaska, following Brent's journey, marking each stop with a black dot. Anchorage to Campbell Airstrip to Willow and Yentna Station and Skwentna and Finger Lake, all twenty-three stops along the way to Nome. It wasn't until after she studied the mileage between each checkpoint that Leslie thought of Dennis for the first time that day. She indulged in the memory of his persistence—the soil and the seeds, the impulsive proposal. She thought of how she'd once won him back with a pile of rotting vegetables, but how she'd failed with a letter about a dead dog. And as she watched Jill draw a large red circle around the notorious Dalzell Gorge and the equally treacherous Farewell Burn, Leslie noted she had never once mentioned the girl in those letters. She was pleased with this fact, and she realized then that she didn't want to show any of this to Dennis.

───

After lunch, Jill went outside and practiced bootying Velma, and Leslie pulled a piece of paper from the stack by the phone and sat down to write a letter.

> Dear Brent,
>
> I hung a yellow ribbon on the tree today, out where Inca died. I couldn't find the sunflowers.
>
> Leslie

She addressed it to the final checkpoint in Nome and walked to the mailbox.

———

On the day Brent was set to cross the finish line, Leslie woke to a barking dog. Shaggy, she thought, more hound than husky. Another joined. Minnow, with that sharp little yelp. And another. Ray Charles, out there crying at all he couldn't see. She followed their calls into the yard and made her rounds. As she carried the bucket to the edge of the property, the aspen trees branched out above her, their trembling leaves like polite applause. When she returned to the yard, the dogs all mounted their houses, lifted their snouts to the open sky, and filled the air with long, dissonant howls. It was as close to a thank-you as Leslie ever got, and she had the irresistible urge to howl back.

# CALL UP THE WATERS

HERE'S WHAT OUR mother told us that summer: beneath our feet was a world of water. Tunnels and tubes ten feet down, thirty feet down, some even further, all bending and merging into rivers and streams. This was the summer of her dowsing rods and pendulums, earth tides and underlands. The summer she twisted wire coat hangers to look like tuning forks and walked up and down the driveway, talking to the ground.

She could find it, she told us. She could find the water.

We weren't the only people she told. She told Joy Cooper, too, who told her husband, Dave. And once Dave knew, Amy Marcus knew. And then Amy told Daniel Rush, who told Mona Towers, who told Lydia Nova. And once Lydia knew, the entire town knew, and for the rest of that summer people took a great interest in our mother.

———

Even in ripped jeans and a dirty T-shirt, her hair knotted on top of her head and held in place by a pencil she'd found between the couch cushions, our mother was the most beautiful woman in town. I have an early memory of her, one I can't place in time, but I see her standing at the kitchen stove in our Colorado home, boiling water until it was safe to drink, storing it in glass jars in cupboards above the sink. Now that she's gone, I think about her every time I see one of those glass jars, the kind people use for canning peaches or chutney or jam.

———

One morning, sometime that summer, my brother, Jack, put a piece of paper in front of me. He lined up his crayons, which he'd just sharpened, and he told me to draw the underground rivers, not from the perspective of a human but from the perspective of an ant. He thought it would help him to understand.

I was eleven, Jack was eight, and while I imagined a ladder into my mother's watery underworld, Jack imagined a set of stairs. When our mother came into the kitchen, her eyes heavy with sleep, her skin pink the way it always was when she woke, she stood behind me, pulling her fingers through my long, thin hair, whispering in her morning voice, "No, no, no, you have it all wrong, my dears."

We waited for her to pick up a crayon and draw it right, but she only sat down with her coffee. Jack and I scrambled for the seat closest to her.

———

Mary-Beth Gates, famous in town for running the same three-mile loop every morning for twenty-five years, suddenly switched her route, finishing her run in the little park across from our house. Jack and I saw her one morning at dawn, stretching her legs for a long time before she finally walked up our stairs and onto the porch.

"Is it true?" she asked. "Can you find us water?"

"Come in, Mary-Beth," our mother said.

The four of us sat down at the kitchen table, the women with their coffee, my brother and I with our orange juice and cereal. We listened as our mother described the world under our feet. Caves. Sinkholes. Buried waterfalls. A raging river that carved tunnels through rock.

Our mother unfolded a map.

"It's here," she said. We all leaned in, and she dragged her finger across the dark green mountains to the west of our town. "All kinds of water in here."

Mary-Beth put her fingers on the mountains. Then she put her whole palm on it and closed her eyes, like she was trying to feel the water. She smiled and said, "Well, if anyone can do it," laughing a little, looking at our mother, who looked at me, and I looked at Jack, who was leaning over himself, tying his shoelaces together. It was a trick we sometimes played on each other, and, when we were really bored, on ourselves. If he could forget about the knot he'd made, he would trip when he tried to walk. But it never worked. We couldn't *not* remember, even when we tried really hard.

<hr />

For two months that summer local farmers siphoned water from the reservoir three hours east until they were caught and fined. People stood in line at the fire station waiting for flats of bottled water, sometimes for hours. They carried empty jugs in their cars in case they were lucky enough to find a spring and set up buckets to collect rainwater, anticipating the late-summer monsoons. When the rain never arrived, the Ingrams packed up and moved to Virginia; the Hazelgroves went to Seattle. Gordon Giles went to live with his son in New Mexico, and eight families on West Ridge Road left together in a train of minivans.

———

Long before all of this, our mother spent her days in her flower beds, tugging weeds with both hands and killing aphids between her fingers. She foraged for mushrooms in the forest behind our house and sold them to our neighbors from the front porch. In our small plot of land, she dug in the soil, pulling out shards of pottery and fish fossils, edible plants she ate without washing. The knees of her pants were mud stained and threadbare, and she could never get her fingernails clean. While everyone else in town checked weather reports each hour and mumbled prayers for rain on Sundays, our mother kept her head down, certain the answer to everything was in the ground.

———

A week after Mary-Beth visited, our mother told us to get in the car. We pulled on our seat belts and she drove us into the canyon, where we climbed high enough and long enough for the radio to cut out and the air to cool, and I thought maybe this time she'd drive us out of Colorado and into Utah like she sometimes promised. Before we reached the state line, the car slowed, and we bumped our way onto a gravel road, wheels throwing pebbles against the underside of the car. I felt the weight of Jack's body against mine, his head on my shoulder. His leg bounced.

I put my hand on his knee. He stopped. All around us were dust and boulders, cliffs and caves. A dry stream. A dead tree.

It hadn't rained in months.

She parked on the side of the road, and we followed her through the forest to a large gash in the side of a mountain. We walked as far as we could with the light from the opening guiding us, and then our mother turned on her flashlight and led us deeper into the darkness until finally she stopped, bent down, and pushed away the dirt with her fingers. Jack and I crouched next to her.

"Here," she said, and we each put a hand where she told us. It was wet. We dug deeper. We reached mud.

"Earth tides," she told us.

She did this. She'd pick up a hobby, busy herself with it for a few months, and before long, it would become an afterthought, an unfinished project that joined all the other unfinished projects. A partial quilt, a half-knitted hat, a birdhouse without a roof, rolls and rolls of photographs never developed. Given time, she'd grow bored of this too, and I knew her dowsing rods would end up in the basket with the knitting needles under the sewing machine she never used.

With all our mother's talk about rivers under our feet, of waterfalls careening into a deep darkness below us, of water rising spontaneously through the hard, hard ground, is it any surprise that Jack was suddenly afraid to leave the house? That he wouldn't step off the front porch without holding my hand because he thought the land might buckle, that the earth might swallow him up, that without a life jacket he'd sink chest deep into an underground river?

———

As she readied for a day of dowsing, we behaved badly because she wouldn't let us go with her. We brought entire tree branches into the living room. We dragged our feet through mud and dirt and leaves and grass, and then we walked into the house and shuffled our feet across the carpet, took off our shoes, and smeared dirt onto the walls. Our mother finally came into the living room, her dowsing bag packed.

"You think I don't know what you're doing," she said. "You think I'll stop everything and scrub the carpets and wash the walls, get everything clean so you can just go out and do it all over again. Well, you'll see. I'll show you."

*Keep going*, we thought. *Let us have it.*

She rounded up every spray bottle, every sponge, every roll of paper towels, every cleaner she could find and put them all in front of us.

"Go on," she said. "I'm not going anywhere until you clean up this mess."

We took our time.

"We can stay here all night," she said.

I ran the sponge over the wood floor, back and forth, back and forth, falling into a rhythm with Jack.

———

One day, I found her in the bed of a dry creek and followed her across the land. Her elbows were pinned at her sides, her L-rods out in front of her, searching for hidden water veins. "What does it feel like?" I asked her. "Is it a pull? A twitch?"

She shook her head. She looked disappointed.

"Of course not," she said. Annoyed, she waved me away, and then she lowered herself to the ground, dropping to hands and knees and then her belly, listening for the world beneath the surface.

———

While Jack was busy worrying about the ground giving out, the underground rivers pulling him down, my own fears were different. I worried she'd call up the waters and they wouldn't stop. They'd keep rising and rising, and we'd be left with a waterlogged home, a drowned cemetery, a rusted skeleton of a car, a church with bells that chimed when the waters were rough. I imagined canoeing over land we'd once used as a garden, fishing in water that had been our front lawn, lake trout moving from my room to Jack's, surveying their new quarters.

———

She taped blank pieces of paper together and spread her canvas from one corner of the kitchen table to the other and stood above it, pencil in hand, tip to page.

"I'm mapping it," she said. "All of it. Every underground tunnel, every turn, every chamber, every spot where the soil is wet."

Mary-Beth arrived, staying the entire afternoon as my mother worked.

As they stood together at the table, the bright sun coming through the window behind them, the light caught my mother's sweat-shined skin and transformed her body into a blur of light. I have seen something similar since then, in dark, crowded restaurants where I live in Boston, a bright light entering the window, framing the body in a deep orange glow. But at the time I didn't realize she was simply backlit, and I began to worry that by mapping the labyrinth under our feet, our mother might ignite.

———

In every other way she was like all the other mothers we knew.

She brushed my hair too hard and too fast. She sent Jack back to the bathroom when she sensed he hadn't flossed. She worried about rising gasoline prices and rising electricity costs, turning the heat low in the winter and flipping off the lights we'd left on in the rooms we were no longer in. She read the newspaper, picked up litter on the sidewalk, insisted we take off our shoes when we entered the house.

———

Except.

A year earlier, before she became a dowser, I found her at the edge of town, arms wrapped around a maple, forehead resting against the trunk. I went to her, certain to drag my feet through the leaves as I approached so I didn't startle her. I rested my hand on her back, and she turned to look at me.

"Chases away bad thoughts," she said, smiling.

We were quiet for a long time, the two of us standing there, my shoes getting lost in the fallen leaves, my mother still holding the trunk.

"Gives me energy," she said. "Life force, you might call it. I've noticed it happens with white pines too. Less so with oaks. Never with sweet gum or sycamore."

"Can we go home now?" I asked.

She took my hand and we walked toward the house, everything quiet except the leaves under our feet.

"I hope it gets something from me," she said. I looked at her, not understanding. "The tree, I mean. I hope it takes something from me."

I could see the little divots in her forehead, the dents from where she rested her face on the bark.

———

Except.

She left us sometimes in the middle of the night because the tides behaved differently when the moon was out. She always waited until she thought we were asleep. I'd hear the creak of the front door, and I'd follow the sound of her heavy boots on the stairs. I'd count each footstep, and when I reached seven, I knew she was gone. Soon after, I'd hear Jack come into my room, and then I'd get out of bed and we'd go to the kitchen.

We ate cereal straight from the box, finished a bag of popcorn and a bag of jelly beans our mother had hidden in the freezer, behind the peas. While we were there, we threw away the peas, and then we tossed the rest of the food we hated. Okra, spinach, broccoli, tuna, cod. We finished off the ice cream and split the last soda. Feeling sick and tired and more than a little scared, we each took an end of the couch and shared a blanket, watching late-night news, waiting for the weather report, fighting about whose feet had crossed the center line.

———

Except.

No other parents skated with their kids, not like she did.

Every winter, when there was still water, someone would pull a rusty steel barrel out into the middle of the lake to signal the freeze-up was over. It was safe to skate. We'd spend hours out there, not just Jack and I but our mother, too. She always looked so comfortable on skates, so pretty. Not pitched forward for balance like me. Never cautious, with her arms out wide, like Jack.

The rest of the parents stood onshore, cheering for their kids as they skated by, pulling their hands out of their pockets occasionally to give a half-hearted wave. But our mother would skate around the perimeter all day, carving a path for herself, never stopping at the middle of the lake to hold the lip of the barrel, or to catch her breath and gather her courage.

Of course, she wobbled where everyone wobbled— on that rough patch of ice under the pine tree—though I only ever saw her fall once, after a slight miscalculation sent her spinning on her butt across the ice. And even that was graceful.

———

That Jack became a pilot never surprised me. Far from the earth he'd once been so scared of. When he first started flying, I was already living in Boston, and he always called me with stories about the routes he'd flown and the views he'd seen. He kept a running list of all the cities he liked most from the air, and then, just a few months later, he was put on a circuit, flying the same route every trip, following the spine of the Rockies away from Denver, up to Calgary, before turning west to Vancouver and then south at the Pacific Ocean. From there he followed the seam of the country to Los Angeles, San Diego, east to Albuquerque, and north again to Denver.

It was a small plane, he told me. It sat thirty people, but sometimes he'd have just two or three passengers at a time, and when that was the case he was always sure to leave the cockpit to welcome them. He understood it could be disorienting to be up so high in a mostly empty plane, especially because the wildfires all over the West had charred pockets of land and turned the skies gray. He wanted to assure them that everything would be okay.

One day when she left us for the earth tides, Jack and I hunted for withered mushrooms we'd seen deep in the forest. Once bright orange, the mushrooms were now brown and flat, hardened to the side of a dead tree trunk. We returned with a bag full of them, but she wasn't there, so we heated the mushrooms in the biggest pot we owned, not bothering to wash or chop them. Then we added a little of everything we could find in the cupboard. Salt and pepper and oregano and a splash of sherry vinegar, balsamic vinegar, white vinegar, red wine vinegar. Peanut oil and flour and baking powder and pancake mix, and then we opened the refrigerator and pulled out the milk and eggs and maple syrup.

We sat across from each other at the kitchen table, marveling at what we'd made, forking the paste up to our noses to smell, holding it to our mouths, cooling it with our fearful breaths.

"Dig in," my brother said, which was what our mother always said.

"Bon appétit," I said, which was what we always said in response.

We sat for a long time, waiting for the other to take the first bite, and then I bent my fork back and let the food fly, flinging it at Jack's face, at the windows, and then we sat in front of the front door, our forks loaded, waiting for it to open. We waited and waited, and when she still didn't return, we took aim at the door.

"That will show her," my brother said.

"Yeah," I whispered, out of breath, hungry.

---

On a different night, we both dreamed we had drowned. Over breakfast we compared our deaths, competing for the most gruesome end, until our mother said, "Enough already."

---

Maybe all the death that summer was just a coincidence. A lizard shriveled on a rock. Honeybees by the dozens, up and down the canyon roads. In our house I noticed it too. Dozens of houseflies in the kitchen window, caught between the screen and the glass. Ladybugs dying in hordes, drifts of them on the doorstep, on the window-sills, in every corner of the cabin. Maybe all these animals would have died anyway. Maybe.

———

"I was never scared of the ground," Jack told me.

We were in Colorado for the final time, back to clean the house and ready it for the market, even though we suspected it wouldn't sell because people had stopped buying homes high in the mountains, surrounded by trees.

Our mother had been dead for three years.

"It was the sky I was always scared of. Don't you remember?"

He reminded me of the news footage we'd seen one of those late nights while we were waiting for the weather report. A journalist asked a weeping man if he knew why the plane might have targeted his house. The man couldn't answer. All he could do was wail at the sky, his arms open, palms up.

"How can you not remember that?" Jack said. "The way the camera zoomed in on his face, how it got way too close?"

I pulled a box from the top of the hallway closet, a collection of my mother's unfinished projects. A water-color with a tree but no sky, a handmade linen jacket with one arm.

"I don't remember any of that," I said. "Are you sure I was there?"

I grabbed the broom and dustpan, gathered the dirt from the closet floor. Outside, I dumped it into the garden, where we used to watch her deadhead the wilted roses.

One day she came home in a state, her face red and her jaw clenched. She wanted us to know she'd walked all the way out past the dry lake and beyond the dead Christmas tree farm before she pulled her bag off her back and found all her tools gone.

"Always," she said. "I always put them in here. Every single time."

She opened her empty bag and showed us. I looked to Jack, who looked to me, and then we both turned to our mother.

"I didn't take them," I said. "Swear it."

"Me either," Jack said.

And our mother wiped at her face, her neck, looking around the house, throwing her tan arms out wide.

"So you're telling me they just disappeared? Just like that?"

She was so pretty when she was mad. Her eyes bigger and bluer somehow, and it was impossible not to stare.

"I guess so," Jack said, and I nodded along.

I mocked her. Just once, but I still mocked her. I was waiting for my friends so we could all climb the fire lookout tower at the top of the hill and throw water balloons from the platform. When they finally came around the corner, I saw the twigs in their hands, their elbows at their sides. They held the sticks just like my mother held her dowsing rods, and they laughed as Owen Carlisle pretended to be dragged this way and that by some invisible force in the ground. When he saw me, he stopped and waited for me to say or do something, and so I did the only thing I could think of. I picked up sticks of my own and ran toward them chanting, in a voice that sounded nothing like my mother, "Water, water, everywhere."

They laughed and laughed.

———

Sometimes when she left us all day and all night, we called her the names we heard Daniel Rush call her: *water witch*, *kook*. Always, when she returned, she whispered in our ears: *My little darlings. My lovely children. My sweet little geese.* She'd help us up from the couch one at a time and lead us to bed, where she'd pull the covers over our shoulders. I loved that feeling of her warm lips against my forehead, her cold hands on my cheek. The smell of soil and grass and rocks and, yes, if I breathed in deep enough, it seemed I could smell fresh water. There, between sleep and awake, I believed her. I thought it was possible that she could find the water with her sticks.

———

Mary-Beth kept returning, not in her running gear but in a thin tank top and loose shorts, her hair pulled back in a knot at the base of her neck. She began to stay longer and longer, through most of the afternoon, studying the map our mother had drawn. "I think it's magical," she would say, her voice full of wonder.

"How do you do it?" I once asked my mother, nodding toward the L-rods on the table.

"Which part?"

"All of it."

"I could teach you."

I thought of Owen Carlisle and how ridiculous he looked imitating her. I shook my head hard. She never offered again, and I never asked.

———

We tried to save her from herself and the embarrassment she was causing. We did everything we could think of.

I told her, "We almost got kidnapped today. By that woman on the corner. She tried to chain us to the telephone pole."

"When you lie," she said, "your left eyebrow goes up. Just a little bit. A small arch."

When she tried to raise her eyebrow, her whole face lifted, and we couldn't help but laugh.

———

Of course I stole her dowsing rods. And the pendulums.

I wrapped everything in a faded floral pillowcase, shoved the entire package in a cardboard box at the back of my closet, and sealed it tight with tape. I stacked two other cardboard boxes on top and labeled each one with giant lies in big black letters: *Photos. Belts. Winter Gear.* I found them years later, when I was packing up all my belongings to move to Boston for college.

I brought the pillowcase to my mother, who was sitting on the couch, making notes about crop rotation for the following spring. She looked inside, smiled.

"I figured it was you," she said, holding them up, her first pair of dowsing rods, metal coat hangers, all twisted and bent.

But I never would have removed the maps. I remember worrying that if I took those and she got out too far, deep into the canyon where she sometimes went alone, she might get lost and not find her way back.

He never admitted it, but I knew Jack had hidden them somewhere, hoping it would be enough to make our mother look up from the ground, to stay home with us.

———

One night, at dinner, she put her mouth to my ear and whispered, in a voice low enough that not even Jack could hear, "Tomorrow."

All night I lay awake in bed, waiting for the daylight, both wanting it and dreading it, worried whatever she had planned would embarrass us further.

When the morning arrived, a dull light came through my window. From my bed I could see the oak tree bending in the wind, and beyond the leaves, I could see clouds, the entire scene blurred from the raindrops on the window. For a long time I stayed in bed, unsure what it meant.

Did she do this? Was it possible? I had always imagined the water coming up out of the ground, but maybe I had it all wrong. I stared at the window and watched the leaves and listened to the rain, and then I got out of bed and walked down the hall to the living room, where my mother and Jack were both on the couch.

"It's raining," I said.

Jack's legs were tucked under his body, his face buried in the pages of a comic book.

"It's raining," I said again.

I sat on the coffee table in front of my mother, and she finally looked up at me, proud and beaming.

All day it rained, not the usual downpour the monsoons dropped at the end of each summer, but a slow, steady drizzle that slicked the roads and soaked the ground. Like everyone else in town, we watched through our windows, relieved it had finally arrived, hopeful it would continue. And it did. Thirty-six hours. Forty-eight. Seventy-two. At some point Mary-Beth arrived, settling into the chair next to my mother at the kitchen table, where once again they studied the map our mother had drawn. They predicted how far the water would travel, how fast it might flow, how long it might last. I moved in as close as I could, listening with a renewed faith, confident now that she wasn't mapping her imagination but charting some invisible world beneath our feet that only she could see or sense.

———

That summer came back to me in a large, dark lecture hall in my final semester of college, when I sat near the front and listened to my geology professor discuss Vitruvius, the Roman architect who thought the best method for finding water was to walk outside before sunrise, lie down on your stomach, rest your chin on the ground, and look for vapors rising and curling together. When you found that, you just had to dig there.

Of course I thought of my mother, of her dowsing rods, her pendulums, how she used to walk through empty riverbeds on hot, bright mornings, and how, tapping into some ancient system of knowledge, she mapped hundreds of miles of underground rivers.

The professor made us understand we were to laugh at the architect's folly, belly down on the ground, searching the horizon for little waves of water.

———

When I first moved to the city, I rode the T around Boston with no place to go or to be, preferring the train lines that mostly ran aboveground to those that traveled below. I loved looking at the buildings, the lights in the windows, the outlines of people in their offices and apartments, so I started to time my rides to coincide with sunset, when people had turned on the lights but hadn't yet closed the blinds. When the train slowed enough for me to see inside their homes, I took note of how they had decorated their walls or arranged their furniture, and then back in my apartment I tried to replicate what I had seen.

Eventually, every train would descend, and a loud sucking sound announced we had entered a tunnel. We'd be deep into the darkness before I realized I was holding my breath.

———

Just before we returned to sell the house, Jack's flight route changed. He didn't travel to new cities; his company reversed the direction of his route. He was to head south from Denver to Albuquerque, and then west to San Diego, north to Los Angeles, and on to Vancouver, before dipping east to Calgary and south again to Denver. He told me how different things looked, especially the roads in the Rockies, which he could see now from the cockpit because new fires had taken out the trees that once hid them.

It seemed as though every time I turned on the news or picked up a newspaper, I found new things to be scared of. It wasn't just the fires in the West, the droughts that didn't end, but stories of downed planes, faulty engines, missing black boxes, airplanes mysteriously disappearing off radar, never to be seen again.

"Honestly," he said, "you have nothing to worry about. Totally different planes. Totally different situations."

Still, I worried, and that night, after we finished boxing the books and Jack went to bed, and the neighbors I had never met turned off their lights, I walked to the small park across the street from the house and put my forehead to a tree trunk. I didn't even know what kind of tree it was. I reached my arms around it. I waited.

The bad thoughts kept coming.

Finally, after what felt like a long time, I released the tree, put my fingers to my forehead, my cheek. I pressed at the dents left by the bark and brushed my arms to remove bits of the tree that clung to me. I laughed. *Ridiculous*, I thought. *Total nonsense.* Every bad thought remained, as stubborn as a drought.

On the day I found out my mother had died—Mary-Beth found her in the kitchen, splayed out on the floor in her pajamas, a pool of blood beneath her head, dripping from a small dent in her temple where she had hit the corner of the counter—I was supposed to move out of my apartment and into a new one on the other side of town. Instead, I packed my suitcase and descended the stairs to the platform, where I waited for the train that would take me under all of Boston and drop me at the airport.

This, of course, was long after she had mapped the water.

After Jack had moved out and Mary-Beth had moved in.

After they had opened the little shop together in town, where they sold guidebooks and maps, dowsing rods and pendulums.

And after they closed the shop because they rarely made a sale.

Standing on that platform, waiting for my train, I missed her with an intensity that frightened me. I hadn't yet cried for her and I wouldn't cry on that platform or in the plane, but I felt a deep sadness, some invisible hand clenching my throat, and without warning, I was back on that frozen lake, gripping the edge of the rusty barrel, watching my mother turn graceful circles, wishing I had that balance.

# THE STONEMASON'S WIFE

JOLINA HAS BEEN hearing voices of men she's never met. Voices like water, clear and cold, eddying at the back of her mind. They're not real. She knows this. As in, she's not crazy. They're only the voices she's heard on the phone, voices of men who buy the magazines she sells or, more often, who don't and instead tell her all the things they could do for her. Low and babbling and swelling voices.

They arrive each night with the darkness, after Barry has gone upstairs, and maybe this is why it feels like a betrayal. A muddying of their marriage. She is here, after all, sitting on the back porch, face to the stars, listening to these strangers while her husband is asleep in their bed.

Jolina isn't always honest with Barry. She doesn't, for example, tell him what the men say. Or that their voices return to her like this. It would only make him worry, and she doesn't like to make him worry. So she tells him that sleep is hard for her. She expects maybe he'll press her to say more. But he doesn't. He only kisses her cheek and says good night, just as he's done each night for five years.

There on the porch, Jolina wraps herself in a blanket and stays up later than she should, long after midnight, watching the stars burn out. She will regret this in the morning at work, when her boss clicks in on the line and hears her stumble over subscription prices and delivery details. But for now she doesn't care. For now, she opens her mind and listens to the men who tell her she has the voice of an angel. That she's too young to sound so sad. That they can make a girl like her happy. If only she would let them. Their voices merge and bend and fall away into the darkness, and still, no matter how long Jolina listens, the voices of women never come to her. This is what surprises her most.

———

Jolina thinks she has slept in the chair on the porch, but now that the sun is up and the sky is light, she isn't entirely sure. She watches the cardinal that is perched on the clothesline, trying to figure out this voice in her head, an old man's voice, the one that keeps saying, *I'm sorry, but I can't.*

The scrape of the kitchen chair sends the bird off, and Jolina remembers that it is Monday, and she's supposed to be getting ready for work.

Inside, Barry is already at the table, a pencil in hand, a piece of paper before him. He stops his scribbling, looks up at her. His hair is a mess, his eyes barely open. He looks disoriented. She loves him. She does.

"A breakthrough?" she asks, sitting down next to him, looking at the piece of paper.

"Maybe," he says. "Can't tell yet."

It happens often for him. An answer to a problem he's been working out for weeks will suddenly appear in his sleep. Not in his dreams. He doesn't dream. Instead an idea is simply there in the darkness, knocking at his brain. This is how he describes it—a knocking. Sometimes

Jolina wakes to find him sitting at the edge of their bed, working out a problem in the margins of the newspaper, or on the side of a tissue box.

Jolina reaches across the table, and Barry opens his hand, ready to take hers, but she leaves it empty and instead pulls the piece of paper toward her.

She doesn't know what this one means. Letters and numbers, intersecting lines. At the top of the page, in capital letters, a single word: *SLATE*.

"You didn't sleep last night," Barry says.

Jolina doesn't look at him. She only shakes her head.

"I sold a magazine subscription to a blind man a few months ago," she says. "He had this really sweet voice, and I could tell he was really old. The voices of older people are different, you know? And he just kept saying, *I'm sorry, but I can't*. But I kept going. Gave him the full sales pitch."

"You can quit that job, Jo."

This is the right thing to say because Barry is her husband and she is unhappy, but it's not true, and they both know it. She can't quit this job because he hasn't worked in nearly two years.

"I kept going on and on," she says, "about how great it would be for him to have a monthly magazine. Like a gift, I told him, it would just show up in his mailbox, and he could read it with his coffee in the morning or with a beer at night, and he told me, clear this time, direct, in this beautiful voice, really sweet, almost apologetic, *I'm blind, Miss*. He called me *Miss*. So then I asked him if he had kids. And he said no, so then I asked him if he had a wife. And he said no again. And then I asked if maybe he had a niece or a nephew or any kids who came over to visit him at his house, and he said yes, there was a young girl from across the street who liked to help him read his mail, and his voice got louder when he talked about her, and I knew then I had him. I told him he could buy a subscription, and then when she came over she could read it aloud to him. And he liked that. I could have stopped right there. But I had to push it. I said, well, what about two subscriptions? Maybe you'd like to buy two because if you get two, then we will donate ten percent to a charity. Any one you choose. And this was a lie. Just made up on the spot because somehow I knew he would say yes. And he just kept saying in the kindest voice, *Yes, I'd like to help. Yes, okay, that sounds okay.*"

Jolina keeps her eyes on the table and waits for Barry to say something, anything. When he is too quiet for too long she looks over and sees that he is staring at the paper in her hands. Without realizing, she has rolled it up into a tube. She unrolls it. Pushes it back across the table to him.

He jots something in the top corner of the paper, folds it into a neat square, and slips it into his pocket.

"It's not forever, Jo," he says. "Lawrence thinks he might have some work for me soon. He thinks come summer he might be able to hire me back full-time."

She has heard this before.

"What are you building?" she asks.

"A wall," he says.

"Another one?"

It's a cruel thing to say, she knows this, and he doesn't respond. Barry is from a family of masons. She believes him when he says it's in his blood, this impulse to stack stones. His grandfather could walk into any house in New England and tell you who built the fireplace. His father could tell you who set the stones on any doorstep. With no work, Barry needs something to do, some way to keep his busy hands moving. But she hadn't expected him to take aim at their yard. A new wall to reinforce the hill at the back of the property. Another to line the garden. Another that seemed to have no clear purpose beyond dividing their yard into two. And another still that divided it into four.

———

That night, Jolina brings new voices home, into their bed. The gravelly voice of the sailor who offers to bring her around the world, who confesses he hopes to die at sea. The businessman who lays out his dreams in such breathless detail Jolina finds it difficult to even keep up with his words. But the voice she is stuck on this evening, the one that is between her and Barry now, the one she falls asleep with, is the surprisingly high voice of the man who cleans the nursing home:

*The nurse,* he said on the phone, *she kept coming in to give the woman food, but the woman thought she had to pay for it. She kept saying,"I don't have money for that. I can't pay for that." In the end I had to pretend I was her date, that I was there to buy her dinner.*

Jolina wakes to a different sound in the middle of the night, the sound of a pencil on paper. She puts her hand on Barry's back.

"Did I wake you?" he says. "I'm sorry. I was trying to be quiet."

His is a nice voice, too, she thinks.

"Was just trying to get this down," he whispers. "Before it's gone."

Jolina can see the form of his body there in the dark, and she wonders what problem it is he thinks he is fixing. She knows in the morning she will find this tiny scrap of paper in the bathroom trash. She knows the answer that had seemed so clear in the middle of the night will turn out to be a dead end, a false start, a misleading glimmer. She will remove the paper from the trash, and she will store it in the top drawer of her dresser, where she has hundreds of other scraps, all lines and angles, equations and lists. Drawings of fireplaces and chimneys and stone walls. Sometimes, when she's home alone, she pulls them all out and lays them on the floor. She tries to understand them. She tries to see what he sees.

He returns to bed beside her. She shifts her body so there is no space between them.

She thought at one point that they had seen the same thing, the day after they married, both barely twenty, when he brought her here to the edge of New England, and showed her this house. One bedroom, one bath. The kitchen barely big enough for a table. Carpets that needed to be replaced and windows that rattled when the wind blew. He took her hand and brought her out back, where ten acres stretched behind the house. Jolina thought then that she could see it. Her entire future. A house of slate walls and limestone floors, granite countertops and marble stairs, her whole life shored up, stabilized with stone.

# BARN BURNING

THE FIRST FLOOR of the Wilcox house served as little more than a passageway. Beyond the tidy mudroom, the clean kitchen, the formal dining room with plates set regardless of the hour, and a sitting room no one ever used was the wide wooden staircase that creaked with each step. The second floor belonged to the Wilcox sisters, Sadie and Rebecca, seventeen and fifteen. Even the bathroom, which sat across from their bedrooms, was never used by their parents, each cupboard and drawer filled with every item a teenage girl might need. Tampons and pads of varying lengths and thicknesses, body sprays for different moods, makeup for different times of day. The den, where every Friday night we watched movies on the giant TV, was decorated with framed posters of Tori Amos, Liz Phair, and PJ Harvey. In the windows hung curtains of wooden beads that clicked pleasantly each time someone parted them. It was from that second floor living room, through the large bay window, that we watched the Wilcox barn burn that New Year's Eve, all of us in agreement about where we last saw Graham Sovich.

I stood at that window, mouth open, waiting for the fire trucks to arrive. Someone was squeezing my hand, and someone else had an arm around my shoulder. My forehead pressed against the cold glass.

"He can sleep through anything," someone whispered.

I was sixteen years old, between the ages of the Wilcox girls, and the newest member of the group. The boys and girls at the party had all grown up together. They'd all kissed one another and held hands, broken up and made out in the back of the movie theater. High school had threatened all of this, just as their parents said it would. They found art or music or science or soccer, new friends in new classes, and then, just as they all rediscovered one another again at the beginning of the school year, I arrived. I didn't ever believe their kindness toward me would last, but for the five months they took me in, I felt for the first time as though I was part of something.

"She's a genius on the piano," Graham told them, introducing me to the rest of them at lunch, just weeks after I moved to town. He called me Liv even though I'd only ever gone by Olivia, and as soon as he said it I thought it might be nice to give the name a try. I sensed then that Graham was the nicest of the group. Like me, he played piano, but he preferred guitar. My arrival and my ten years of private lessons removed the expectation and the burden that he would play in the orchestra. It also meant he could pursue his real musical dream of becoming a lead singer and guitarist.

He played me recordings of him singing into the tape deck—acoustic versions of his favorite rock songs, rock versions of his favorite ballads—and then he asked me what I thought. I told him he was a better singer than he was a guitarist, and he said he was grateful for my honesty. He told me this while he was sitting on the edge of my bed, me standing in front of him, between his legs, his hands on my hips, my parents downstairs watching *Jeopardy!*, the sounds of their voices rising up the stairs as they shouted wrong answers at the television. I wished then my parents weren't so loud or so wrong or so committed to watching *Jeopardy!* every night at seven. After Graham kissed me for the first and only time, my lips closed, his open, his tongue wet and hot against my mouth, he thanked me for coming to town and I awkwardly thanked him back. When a new song came on the stereo, Graham kept his hands on my hips and nodded toward the speaker.

"My favorite singer of all time," he said of Bob Dylan, and then he asked me which of Dylan's songs was my favorite. When I hesitated he gave me options.

"'Tangled Up in Blue'? 'Not Dark Yet'? 'Like a Rolling Stone'?"

I was ashamed not to know any of those songs, and so I named the only one I could remember. Graham laughed and told me that was the Beatles.

On the night of the kiss, as I tried to sleep, I couldn't get the image of him out of my mind—him smiling, his teeth a little yellow and filmy, his gums red and puffy, like they were on the verge of opening up, bleeding. His eyes and hair were nice enough, I thought, and his pale skin wasn't marked with the bumps and pimples so many of the boys had. But I felt bad for how little I liked looking at him and worse that I had agreed to see him again because I understood he was my doorway into this world. After being mostly invisible for sixteen years, it seemed a small price to pay. I just had to try a little harder to like him.

After that, Sadie Wilcox, the older of the two Wilcox sisters, started to invite me to parties. She let me borrow clothes from her closet, which, months after she had bought them, still had tags. She told me stories about their trips to Costa Rica and Guatemala, and she taught me Spanish words as we sipped from miniature bottles of liquor that she had taken from the planes. She brought me souvenirs when they traveled to these faraway places, and she told me about movies she had watched on the flights, always listing the names of the actors and directors as though they were her friends. I believed it was possible they were.

In the middle of the night that the barn burned with Graham Sovich inside, Sadie Wilcox stood at the window next to me. It was her hand that was squeezing mine, and her fingers, like mine, were cold. Before this, when we had been woken to the light of the burning barn, we ran outside and stood there in front of it, barefoot and without coats, calling Graham's name, holding on to one another, fighting the urge to go in to get him. Ultimately, we gave in to Mr. Wilcox, who had pushed us all inside and told us to stay there. So we watched from that upstairs window as the volunteer fire trucks stalled on the ice that covered the long, steep driveway. There wasn't another house for miles. This was Maine. The nearest town was thirteen miles away.

On the driveway the volunteers gave up trying to get their truck up the ice and instead dragged a hose as close as they could to the flames. They kept falling and getting back up. Mr. and Mrs. Wilcox were outside, trying their best to help. More volunteers arrived, and since they couldn't maneuver their truck past the first, the driver and passenger stumbled and slipped their way up the driveway on foot. Behind them, the barn burned, flames high enough and bright enough that when I looked to my right I could see Sadie's face clearly although there were no lights on. Her hair was pulled back from her face, held in place by her New Year's tiara.

"You wouldn't even open your mouth for him," Sadie said. She loosened her grip on my hand, and she wiped at her face. I'd never told her he had kissed me, but I'd always assumed she knew.

Someone told me to close the blind, which I did. There must have been ten others there that night, maybe more—at least a few girls who had once called Graham a boyfriend, a few boys who claimed he was like a brother. They were huddled together on the floor or the couch, consoling one another, hands on shoulders, arms around waists. Someone turned on the overhead light. One boy, who rarely spoke and never to me, sat alone in the corner, weeping loudly into his arms, which were smeared black from smoke and ash.

"I tried," the boy said. "I tried to get him to come inside."

"Are we even sure he's out there?" I asked him.

"His parents," someone said. "They're in New York."

"No," someone else said. "They're in Boston."

We had all heard Graham just hours before insist he would sleep out in the barn, as we had all planned at the beginning of the night. We would sleep out there this year and next year, Graham said, and we would all return home from college every year that followed to sleep out there because it was to become a tradition for the group, proof that no matter how far we went from one another, we would always come back. Graham got sentimental when he was drunk, and even though we had all agreed to the plan earlier that night, the temperature had dropped, the fire in the woodstove had burned low, it had started to sleet outside, and the house, with the heat on, was just across the driveway. He asked me to sleep next to him, in the sleeping bag he had laid out behind the woodstove, and instead of answering him I went to find another drink. He didn't ask me again, but he did make his way around the room, drink in hand, whispering in the ear of one girl and then another before settling in front of Sadie, who didn't walk away and who smiled at whatever he'd said.

Sadie stood by the window now, running her hands through the beaded curtain. I wanted her to stop.

Another truck pulled up—a real fire truck—and I heard firemen outside on the driveway giving commands, and then I heard Mr. Wilcox explaining that he lived here, that this was his property, that there might be a kid in there. Sadie finally stopped with the beads when Rebecca came up the stairs and went to her side.

"Dad will lose his license over this," she said.

"Rebecca's right," Will said. "They'll find the alcohol, the weed. Your dad could lose his practice. It's true." Will's father was a lawyer, and it was Will who always updated us on the legal consequences of our fun.

Mr. Wilcox was an orthopedic surgeon, and he was also, of all our fathers, the only one who would look the other way when we promised there would be no drugs, just music and a gathering, a ringing in of a new year with good friends. We wanted to use the barn, and he excitedly told us about the woodstove that still worked, the one they had stored in the barn after a remodel of the living room. He always thought it would come in handy, and he could get us electricity out there, too, to hang a strand of Christmas lights. Mrs. Wilcox, he had suggested, could make us cider and soup to keep us warm. Mr. Wilcox wasn't naive. Rather, he wanted to be liked by his children and their friends. He was handsome and charming. He had been popular in high school, and he wanted to be popular still. I was certain we had him to thank for the peach schnapps.

Sadie turned from the window and looked at me. Her makeup was smeared around her eyes.

"You're a tease," she said, jabbing her finger into my chest.

Rebecca tried to grab her sister's arm, but Sadie kept jabbing, saying it again and again. Others helped pull her away. Most of them watched, sitting quietly.

"You're a tease. And everyone will know," Sadie said. Someone led her down the hallway. "You should have been out there," she yelled.

———

After Graham kissed me, I went with him to see his cousin play baseball, hoping the rest of the group would be there. When they weren't, I sat next to him on the bleachers while his parents stood at the fence yelling for the cousin, who stole three bases and hit a double. I thought maybe Graham would introduce me to them when the game was over, but instead he suggested we leave after the sixth inning. He'd found this great spot to watch the sunset; he could drive me home after, he said. I told him I needed to get home and that I wanted to walk. He said it was too far and much too cold, but I pulled the sweatshirt out of my bag and told him I liked the exercise. This was around the time everyone in our group had started kissing one another on both cheeks when we said goodbye. I kissed Graham on the left cheek and then on the right, and I felt his hand move from my waist to my ribs to the side of my chest. No boy had ever touched me like that, and I held my breath until he dropped his arm and said he'd walk me out to the road at least. He stood up and made his way down the bleachers. We walked away from the cheering, and it felt like I was supposed to say something, so I asked where everyone else was. Sadie, Rebecca, the others. Graham shrugged, said he didn't know, and put his arm around my waist, pulling me toward the short-cut through the woods. I felt him tugging at my shirt, and then I felt his fingers on my skin, searching for the edge of my jeans. He talked as he did it—mostly about his cousin, the pitcher, who had struck out nine in a row, who was looking at his first shutout of the season—and I tried to move away, but he had a good grip. By the time we reached the road, he'd slipped his fingers under the top edge of my underwear, found my hip bone.

"Aren't you curious?" he whispered, his hand reaching further. "Just a little bit? Don't you wonder?"

My throat tightened. "Your hands are really cold."

On the walk home, I stopped at the pharmacy and bought a pregnancy test. I went straight to the bathroom before I said hello to my parents. There were two in the box. I followed the instructions on the back. I knew I couldn't get pregnant without having sex. I knew that, but I pulled out the second test just in case the first had lied.

———

Down the hall, I heard Rebecca trying her best to calm Sadie down. I went to them. I knocked even though the bedroom door was open. No one invited me, but I entered anyway. Sadie was pulling items out of my backpack—clothes she had given me just weeks before, a pretty blue skirt, a sweater, a bracelet. Everyone was piled on the bed, looking not at me but at Sadie, their limbs entangled, legs where arms should be, arms under bodies. Sadie sat on the edge of the bed. Someone twirled her hair. I went over and tried to take a corner. Someone extended a leg to prevent me from joining them.

I returned to the wall and slid down it until I was sitting on the carpet, and I could feel the warmth against my legs. Heated floors. I hadn't known such a thing existed until the first night I'd slept in this house. I sat there now while the rest of them huddled on the bed, and I knew something about this scenario was pathetic, that I was pathetic for staying there as the red lights flashed in the windows and the firemen shouted to one another. I have no idea how much time passed like this, but at some point the red lights stopped flashing, the light in the windows began to change from black to blue, and I shifted my legs, and everyone on the bed turned to look at me as though they had just woken up and were surprised to see me still there.

No one tried to stop me when I left. I descended the wooden stairs, each one creaking louder as I made my way further from the second floor. I walked through the formal dining room, where I once ate mussels in a spicy red sauce with Mr. and Mrs. Wilcox while Sadie and Rebecca, vegetarians, poked at their salads. In the kitchen, Mrs. Wilcox stood at the sink, staring out at the barn that had finally stopped burning. If she saw me come into the room, she didn't acknowledge it. She scrubbed her hands and arms, which I could see were covered with soot and ash.

"You're welcome here any time," Mrs. Wilcox had said at the end of the first weekend I stayed with them. She had pulled me close for a hug, and a bit of her hair made its way into my mouth. My mother used the same shampoo. It was a fact that gave me a disproportionate sense of joy.

I continued outside without saying goodbye to her. I could see that icicles had already started to form around the empty windows of the barn. Everything from the evening before—the couch where we had taken group pictures, the Christmas lights we had strung up, the party hats and tiaras, the beer bottles and liquor bottles—it was all gone. The only thing spared was the woodstove.

I walked down the driveway toward Mr. Wilcox, who stood with his arms crossed over his chest, legs spread wide, talking with two firemen, all of them staring at the destruction. I assumed they were speaking about the tragedy of it all, the absolute devastation of the night that had just played out in his backyard. But as I got closer, I heard him inquire about their knees. Were they feeling better? Did they have full range of motion? Was physical therapy helping? They answered, much too enthusiastically. Never felt better. I thought Mr. Wilcox might see me as I approached, and that he might put his arm on my shoulder, the way he did when he said hello to me and goodbye. But no one seemed to notice me.

*Tease.* The word followed me down the icy driveway to my car. I had parked on the dirt road so no one would be able to see from the Wilcox house that my father had fixed the bumper with duct tape or that I had tried to paint the tape black to match the car. On the way down, I passed Graham's parents, summoned from Boston or New York or wherever they had been, who were trying to run up the icy driveway toward the scene behind me. They were holding hands, trying to stay on their feet.

———

Of course everything changed afterward. How could it not? A boy had died. My father, not typically one to express emotion, told me daily that he loved me, which I could tell my mother made him do and made him uncomfortable. My mother seemed torn—beyond glad to have me around so much, alive, here, and yet also worried about why I insisted on being alone. To comfort her I tried to seem busy, which meant I became for the first time in my life a diligent student of the piano. I ran my fingers up and down the scales, practiced arpeggios, taking care not to let my hands or fingers collapse. I played

Chopin's Scherzo no. 2 until I'd perfected the passage-work. Sometimes my parents stood at the door watching me. I never looked up at them. I couldn't bear to see their faces. To see them smile at me. To see them proud of me at a time like this.

The remaining six days of winter break dragged. I wanted nothing more than to return to school so I could see Sadie. I tried to call her twice, and each time the phone rang eleven times, and then I remembered they had an answering machine that told them who was calling. Since she refused to answer my calls, I put myself in places where she would see me. I offered to go grocery shopping with my mom because Sadie often went with her mother. I sat in the overstuffed chairs near the front door at the public library, the cold wind hitting me hard every time someone entered. Sadie was an avid reader—it was one of the many things I admired about her—and I hoped to catch her on her way in as she returned books. I wanted to tell her. I wanted to tell her how I'd let Graham lift my shirt in the woods, slip his hand into the front of my pants. I checked twice to make sure I had the pregnancy test in my backpack. I wanted to show it to her. I'd tell her how I saw the principal coming out of the pharmacy just as I had been going in, how humiliating it would have been had he seen me paying for the test at the counter. I imagined how she would look at me in surprise. How she would take my hand. Hug me. Apologize for making me go through it alone.

When the library finally closed, I walked home with a strange sensation that the night might extend forever, on and on, achingly slow. My heart pounded in my chest even though I wasn't walking fast, and by the time I turned down my street, I found it difficult to breathe. I thought maybe I was dying. I wondered if this was what it had felt like for Graham. I considered knocking on my parents' door to wake them, but instead I sat down at the piano. I set my metronome and played the scherzo at half speed. When I could breathe again, I turned the metronome up, little by little, until I was playing the piece faster than it would ever be played in a performance. I played until my wrists ached and until my father came into the room.

"Come on," he said. "It's time to rest."

"I'm not tired," I said.

"Well, the rest of us are."

———

The next morning, the day of Graham's funeral, I woke up with a sore throat. It hurt to brush my hair and my teeth. The soles of my feet burned. I swallowed medicine from the cabinet above the sink, and though it eliminated the pain in my throat, it left me feeling like I was floating as I stood at the back of the packed church with my parents. The entire town showed up. Every pew was full. I could see the back of Sadie's head at the front of the church. Her father offered the final eulogy. He spoke of Graham's optimism. His commitment to his friends. His athleticism: soccer, basketball, baseball. Then Mr. Wilcox pledged financial support for a music scholarship in Graham's name. He promised so much money the couple standing next to me gasped, and I understood then he would never lose his license or be blamed for the barn fire.

The next day, our first back at school, was the only day Sadie and I shared a class—a first-period study hall. I crawled out of my bed and into the shower, hopeful the hot water would loosen my throat and make me look less sick. I used my mother's foundation to cover the dark spots under my eyes. Put on extra blush. Dried my hair so it was straight and soft. Downstairs, my mother touched my forehead and rubbed her fingers up and down my neck, under my ears. I insisted I felt better than I looked, and after hesitating, she agreed I could go to school.

Sadie came into study hall just as the bell rang, wearing a sweater I had never seen before, white with blue flowers around the neckline. Her eyes were puffy. She wiped her nose with a tissue, and at first I thought she too might be sick, and this was the reason she hadn't returned my calls or gone to the library or the grocery store. I immediately felt relieved and hopeful, and I smiled at her when she sat down next to me. She barely looked at me. She opened a book and put it on the desk in front of her. She pulled out a piece of paper and a pen. I thought for sure this meant she would write me a note, the way she normally did in study hall. Thirty minutes passed like this, and I pretended to care a lot about the history textbook in front of me, flipping the pages slowly, reading every caption. Finally, I pulled out a piece of paper from my backpack.

*It's nice that your parents are starting that scholarship.*

I passed it across the desk when the study hall proctor wasn't looking. Sadie read it but didn't touch it. The paper sat in front of her. When the bell rang, the other students packed up. The study hall proctor left, and then it was just me, Sadie, and a freshman boy who took a long time putting away his books. When the boy finally finished, he threw his backpack over his shoulder and ran out of the room. I looked at Sadie. She was crying.

"Oh my god," I said.

What I remembered then: the way she stood next to Graham after he'd made his way around the party that night. How she didn't flinch when his mouth got close to her ear. How she pushed her hair away from her neck and smiled when he handed her a drink. How effortless it looked when she tipped the drink to her mouth, and how, after handing it back to him, she rested her hand on his shoulder, slid it down his back, whispered something in his ear.

"You promised him you'd go back out there," I said, suddenly sad for her. "That's why he stayed in the barn."

Outside the classroom, someone slammed a locker shut. Someone else shouted down the hall for a girl named Edith. Finally, her eyes watery and red rimmed—I swear I saw this—Sadie nodded just once. I reached across the void between our desks and tried to grab her hand, but she was out of her seat and headed for the door before I could touch her.

Before lunch, the nurse took one look at me and insisted on calling my mother, and at the doctor's office later that afternoon the physician told me the test had come back positive. I had mono.

"Who have you been kissing?" she asked me. I wanted her dead.

She gave me a prescription for steroids. My mother brought me home, put me in bed, and covered me with a pile of blankets. I felt both awful and relieved to be under so much weight.

I remembered the next three days in flashes—a sip of tea, a taste of broth. I kicked my covers off and pulled them back on. My mother brought me food I couldn't eat. My father moved the small TV from the kitchen to my bedroom. I thought surely Sadie would hear how sick I was. She would come over, sit beside me on my bed. We would compare stories of all the times we'd said no to Graham, all the times we wished we had said yes.

Maybe the Wilcox family said it aloud over dinner once in a while, tried it out to see how it sounded—"That Liv, where has she been?" Mr. Wilcox might say. But then Mrs. Wilcox would pass him the potatoes, mention the roasted garlic she'd added this time, the heavy cream and horseradish. And that's all it would take to be forgotten.

But I was no better. I told myself I missed Graham—every night I told myself that. I told my mother that, and my father. I used him as an excuse so I didn't have to come out of my room. Some nights I even listened to the cassettes he had given me, trying to make myself feel something other than relief that I hadn't been in the barn and that Sadie hadn't either. I would slip the tapes into my Walkman and listen to Graham—his voice pitch-perfect, his fingers clumsy and a little sloppy on the strings—and remember how each morning at school he would find me at my locker and ask: *Did you listen? What did you think? Did it blow you away?*

When I finally felt well enough to join my parents at the table for breakfast, my mother told me she had seen Graham's mother in town.

"She asked about you," my mother said.

"What do you mean?"

"She wants you to come over when you feel up to it."

"What for?"

"I don't know," my mother said. "She said she has something to give you."

I swirled blueberries into my yogurt.

"Did Sadie call?" I asked.

"Who?" she said.

I shook my head.

"Never mind."

I ate a spoonful of yogurt. I swallowed. For the first time in days I noticed an absence of pain.

———

The house smelled like Graham. Or rather he had smelled like it.

I followed Mrs. Sovich slowly down the long hallway as she stopped at each picture to narrate every moment of Graham's life. Graham at five, his first school picture, toothy and goofy, a wild head of curly brown hair. Graham at ten, soccer practice. His first recital. His last recital. It took us fifteen minutes to get through the hall of pictures, and then the house opened up into a living room crowded and messy with memories: paintings Graham had made in kindergarten, bicycles he had drawn in middle school. Pottery made in art class.

Boxes and bags lined the walls. Flowers in vases had started to wilt. She pushed the clutter around on the table, looking for something. I was standing quietly near the door, eager to leave once she had found what she wanted to give to me, when I noticed the television in the corner had been paused. Graham stood alone on the screen in his soccer uniform, his face red, his hair slicked with sweat.

Mrs. Sovich must have seen me looking at it, because soon she was rushing me to that side of the room, moving things off the couch, insisting I sit down and watch with her. "The local station is doing a feature story on him," she said. "They asked me to have a look." She retrieved a glass of water for me and a cup of tea for herself. She hit play and Graham's laugh came through the TV speakers. His father kept saying *a little higher, a little higher*, until a trophy topped with a soccer player was next to his face. Then the video cut to the room we were now sitting in— the Sovichs' living room—where Mr. and Mrs. Sovich held up pieces of Graham's childhood.

"His favorite color was blue," Mr. Sovich said, speaking into the camera. He brought the cameraman out to the garage to show them the blue bike and blue skis. He loved blue bubble gum as a kid. He would only eat blue lollipops, blue popsicles. "The first year he played baseball he insisted on a blue bat, a blue glove, even though he was on the Red Sox."

The video cut to footage of Graham, seven years old, hitting a ball off the tee, running the bases, pausing near second to pick up something in the grass before continuing onward, all while the players on the other team chased the ball, overthrew it, fought over it. Graham made it all the way to home plate before he tripped over his own feet and collapsed. His teammates ran out of the dugout. They piled on him in celebration. I sipped at the glass of water, wanting both to leave and to stay. I wanted to see if I was in the video. I wanted to see what they said about the fire. I wanted to see pictures of the barn. I waited to see who they blamed.

Sadie and the others appeared only once, when they looked to be in middle school, standing at the front of a classroom, dressed in matching pumpkin costumes. Pictures of Graham in a high chair, then in the front seat of his car, flashing his license. Graham in a backpack on his mother's chest, then with his own backpack hanging off his shoulders on his first day of kindergarten. Graham as a baby in his father's lap, sitting at the piano, and then footage of his last recital. The video lingered there, and I couldn't help but notice how his shoulders slumped, how his wrists collapsed, how lazily he picked his way through Schumann's *Waldszenen*, a piece I could play from memory. He missed notes, ignored all dynamics, playing the loudest parts too soft and the softest parts too slow. The video only showed him once with his guitar, sitting on his bedroom floor in a blue beanbag chair, smiling into the camera. Before the picture flashed off the TV, I saw the small tape recorder beside him. The final shot was a black screen with the dates of his birth and death.

Mrs. Sovich remained on her side of the couch, her hands shaking, her tea spilling over the edge of her cup onto the floor. She stared straight ahead at the black screen. Upstairs, someone opened a door, exited a room, entered another, closed the door. A flush, the faucet, a door opened, closed again. I waited for Mr. Sovich to come down, but when he didn't appear I cleared my throat and finally Mrs. Sovich looked at me.

"Right," she said, wiping her face. "Of course. You must be going." She stood up and went to the piano in the corner of the room where she stood for a moment, her back to me. A sound escaped her, something between a scream and a sob, and then she coughed twice, trying to cover it up. After another moment, she returned to me with a black folder in her hands.

"He always talked about how talented you are," she said, handing me the folder. "He was heartbroken when you got the spot in the orchestra, but he told me again and again how much you deserved it."

I opened the folder. It was sheet music.

"We were hoping you might play something at the benefit concert," she said. "Anything from here would be wonderful, although Graham was, as I'm sure you know, particularly fond of the nocturnes."

I wanted to tell her the truth: he hated Chopin. He hated the piano. He planned to quit as soon as he graduated high school. He vowed never to touch the thing when he went to college. But myth is easier than truth, and myths about dead boys the easiest of all, and so I took the music and put my water glass in the kitchen sink. When I returned Mrs. Sovich was back on the couch. She pressed at some buttons on the remote, and the video started again from the beginning. I let myself out.

———

I returned to school. Between fifth and sixth periods, I saw Sadie standing in front of my locker, fiddling with the lock. We had each other's combinations, and we often left gifts for each other between classes. I watched her as she placed something in there, closed the door, and then walked the other way, down the stairs, heading to chemistry class. I knew she would be late if she didn't hurry, and so I didn't try to stop her. Instead, I clicked through the combination. What did I expect to find? She often left me notes. Pieces of jewelry she made. A book she thought I might like. Instead, I found a dark rock the size of my palm, and I thought maybe her family had taken a trip. Perhaps this was why she hadn't visited. A lava rock from Hawai'i, I thought; she was always talking about Hawai'i. When I picked up the rock it broke into two. A black powder coated my fingers. I realized it wasn't a rock at all but a wedge of charred wood. A piece of the barn.

For the next three weeks this continued, small offerings left in my locker. A thin, warped wire I assumed was from Graham's guitar. A piece of rubber, maybe from his shoe. The items were meant to hurt me, even to scare me. But they didn't. Each day, I collected all the small pieces of him, wiped them clean of soot and ash, and lined them up on the windowsill beside my bed until the collection became too big and I moved it to the top of my dresser. When I undressed at night, it felt as though I was undressing in front of him, like he was watching me, like his hand was on my hip, slipping further and further down, and I thought *yes*.

My invitation to the benefit concert said to wear Graham's favorite color—blue—but instead I wore what I always wore when I performed, a long black dress that touched the floor, a black cardigan to cover my shoulders. I sat through multiple performances, each a tribute to Graham in some way. His favorite Bach piece. His favorite Brahms. Mr. Wilcox had called in a favor with a friend in Boston, and a man came from the New England Conservatory to perform a commissioned piece, a technically demanding solo that ended with a frenzied ascent, delivering an abrupt stop to a dazzling beginning. Or at least this was what the concert program said. In case anyone in the audience missed the parallel, Mr. Wilcox took to the stage to thank his friend and to explain to everyone that the piece was meant to evoke Graham's truncated life.

Mr. Wilcox was trying so hard. He insisted on taking the microphone at the end of each piece to say something about it, and I suddenly felt embarrassed for the Wilcox family. They were all sitting together in the front row. They had organized the event. They had paid to have Graham's piano brought from his childhood home to the auditorium. They had designed the program, printed it themselves. They priced the tickets at a hundred and fifty dollars each, with all proceeds going to the scholarship in Graham's name. Sadie and Rebecca were there with their parents, and my parents were at home, certainly scoffing together at the nerve of the man. A hundred and fifty dollars each. Three hundred dollars total. They didn't want to go anyway, they told me, but I knew they were lying. We just couldn't afford it.

Mr. Wilcox introduced me as Graham's good friend and piano partner, and I took to the stage. I gave a small, quick bow, the way I had been taught, and then I sat down on the piano bench where I knew Graham had sat

miserably for so many years. I could have played the nocturnes. Even without the sheet music I could have played
them from memory. It was what everyone was expecting.
It was what the program said I would do. But instead of
placing my fingers on the keys, I closed the keyboard cover
and took out a small tape recorder I had in my pocket. I
reached for the microphone Mr. Wilcox had been using,
and I held it up to the speaker of the recorder. I hit play.

When the music came on, I watched Mr. and Mrs.
Sovich, who sat in the front row. I hoped they would recognize the sound of the guitar, the fingerpicking of the
opening bars. But it wasn't until the first pitch-perfect
note—that voice of a ghost—came through the microphone that Mrs. Sovich turned to look at her husband.
His lips parted. He rested his hand on his wife's leg.
Recognition rippled through the rest of auditorium.
Everyone turning to one another to help confirm that
they were hearing what they thought.

Graham had given me the recording the day after I
didn't kiss him. It was the Beatles song I had mistaken
for Bob Dylan. He'd asked what I thought of his version,
and because I was still trying to convince myself to like
him, I told him it was even better than the original. What
was true: he sounded even more like himself in the auditorium, his voice bigger, his words clearer, and I brought
the microphone closer to the small speaker. I watched
Sadie, there in the front row, her mother next to her, her
sister on the other side, all of them staring up at me. It
was my offering to her, my answer to those charred pieces
of the barn she'd been leaving in my locker, all I had to
give her. I wondered if she felt anything when she heard

his voice and whether it was the same thing I felt—a distant grief, a small note of quiet sadness, barely audible, but there, deep in my chest. Sadie didn't look away from me until Graham's mom let out one of her awful noises—a loud sob, wet with tears, drowning out her son's voice. Her husband tried to soothe her, but for the last two minutes of the song, it was clear no one was listening to Graham's voice, or his masterful fingerpicking near the end, or the interesting way he dropped into a minor key in the last bar. Everyone was listening to his mother sob. That's what everyone heard.

When the song was over, I put the recorder in my pocket, placed the microphone back on the stand, and made my way off the stage. As I walked to my seat, I knew everyone was looking at me. Mr. Wilcox, it turned out, had nothing to say about my performance, and instead he quickly introduced the next performer, who was to play the final piece of the night. I don't remember who it was or what he played, but I do remember that when he sat down at the piano, he had to push up the keyboard cover before he began.

I sat alone with my little note of grief, waiting for the night to be over. When the music finished and the audience was thanked, I walked up the aisle toward the door, and I felt a hand on my shoulder. A man I had never met thanked me. He said he had always loved that song and was happy to know Graham could play the guitar. He patted my shoulder, and then he was gone into the crowd, headed toward the group that had gathered near the stage. Sadie stood between her parents, arms crossed, looking around the room. When her eyes found me, I waved. She didn't wave back, and as I left, I thought that the four of them—huddled in their tight circle, arms crossed over their chests, none of them looking at one another—were maybe the saddest family in the entire town.

I have always been grateful for the stranger who approached me that night, since, later, people would tell my parents that my stunt had ruined the evening, that it was entirely inappropriate. To bring a boy back like that. Without any warning.

———

Over the years, Graham returned in strange ways: sometimes as a teenage boy, the one who tugged at my shirt and reached for my skin, but more often as the child I had seen on that video while sitting on his parents' couch. It happened when my own daughter came into the kitchen one evening to tell me a little boy was outside on the curb. I was cutting red peppers and told her I was too busy and maybe she could just use her words to describe him for me. But she pulled me to the window anyway. It was nearly night, and on the corner under the maple tree sat a child, his feet in the road, his head resting on his knees. I knew what I saw was just a bag of sand, half full, there since the winter when I had to deal with the icy sidewalks. I didn't have the strength or the desire to drag it back to the shed, so I left it there. But my daughter was right. In this light, from this angle, it looked like a child.

"His name is Patrick," my daughter said. It was the time in her life when everything was named Patrick—her stuffed bear, her hamster, a favorite utensil.

I watched the shape late into the night. I imagined

inviting him in, coaxing him up off the curb to the kitchen table. I imagined serving him a bowl of soup. Some hot cider. I imagined keeping him, setting him up in the guest room at the end of the hall, which we could paint blue. But I knew by the slump of his plastic shoulders, the way his arms fastened under his legs, that he wouldn't be the kind of boy to trust a woman with soup and warm drinks.

Near the end of summer, my daughter came into the bathroom to tell me that Patrick was dead. She was crying in that way that made her lose her breath. I wrapped myself in a bathrobe and brought her with me to the window in the living room, where I saw the bag had fallen over, pounded down by a rainstorm. I went outside in nothing but a bathrobe and slippers, and a neighbor walked by with his dog while I adjusted the bag so it sat as it had before. I returned to the house, and my daughter and I moved from room to room, standing at every window, assessing the scene from every angle. We tried to see what we saw before, but it was still just a plastic bag. The boy was gone.

# BENDING THE MAP

THE MORNING OF the annual Mt. Baldy race, I looked up from the dirt road at the void in the canyon wall where my cabin should have been. Behind me, runners in breathable shirts and matching hats trotted by. They couldn't have known that it was my cabin that had slipped from the canyon wall the night before, that the remnants of my house and all my belongings had washed down the river. They couldn't have known this, yet I still resented their voices. Fathers coaching daughters, husbands and wives breathing in sync, all of them beginning the seven-mile, four-thousand-foot climb with annoying joy.

I climbed too. Not with the runners, and not to the top of the mountain. I climbed sixty-four stone steps so I could pound on my neighbor's front door. When Peter answered, he was wearing only his underwear.

"It's you," he said.

"You've got my safe."

He ducked his head under the doorframe. I focused on his collarbone.

"Come in," he said.

"My safe."

"After you come in for breakfast."

"That's blackmail."

Behind him something shrieked.

"American kestrel," he said. "A student brought it in yesterday. Broken wing and a leg all mangled. He keeps trying to fly, so I had to tie him down."

Peter was an adjunct at the community college at the base of the mountain. He taught a single class called Skulls and Teeth, but only because they wouldn't let him teach one on falconry. For my birthday he nailed a bird skull to my front door while I was out on a search and rescue. He said its empty eye sockets were shaped like hearts. When Andrew and I returned that night, I took it down even though I could feel Peter watching me through his binoculars. Later, after Andrew and I had toasted our rescue—a young girl and her mother who'd made a wrong turn on Ice House Canyon Trail—he undressed me, and I remember being grateful for the oak outside my bedroom window, its thick canopy of leaves shielding us from Peter's gaze.

The kestrel called again, but instead of going to it, Peter showed me his fist. It was covered in scratches. He opened his fingers to reveal something red and glistening. A bird heart, I thought.

"Have to serve him raw beef. It's all I have."

"Give me my safe."

He opened the door wider to welcome me in, but I turned and started back down the front steps.

"I'll be back with Andrew," I said.

The steps were slick with pine needles, making my departure slower than I wanted. Ten steps down, I saw a man run by wrapped in an American flag. His friend wore the California state flag like a cape. There were always a few every year who raced rogue, who took the more challenging climb in less time and with no aid stations. They always dressed up; last year someone in a banana costume overheated a mile from the summit.

Something hit my shoulder. Then the back of my knee. My hip.

"Come back," Peter said.

"Are you throwing pine cones at me?"

"Don't get Andrew. Just come back. I'll give you your stuff."

I climbed back up the steps and onto his porch.

"I'll wait here," I said.

"I'm sorry. About your cabin."

I said nothing, only looked down at my pants, which were covered in mud.

"You look cold. Come in while you wait."

I had spent the first hours of the day wading through the river, crawling through heavy brush, searching for whatever was left of my possessions. I could feel my feet shriveling in my wet socks. My fingers ached with cold.

"Only if you get decent," I said.

He gestured to the chair next to the fireplace, but I stood by the coatrack instead as he disappeared down the hall.

Even with a row of skulls staring at me from the mantel, it felt like home. Every cabin on the road had the same floor plan, with the bathroom and bedroom down the long hall, the kitchen adjacent to the living room, and a small front porch suspended over the edge of the canyon road. I had been here once before, on the night Andrew found those three missing boys at the bottom of a canyon. It was my night off. I'd grown used to the thwacking of the helicopters, and when I no longer heard them I went to the only other place with lights still on.

I studied the index cards taped beneath each skull: scrub jay, raccoon, coyote, mouse. I picked up the raccoon skull and flipped it over to find six molars still in their sockets and a canine dangling loosely at the front of the mouth. I pulled it out, put it back. I pulled it out again and left it on the mantel, next to the other fragments of bone and beak. A single skull on the end hadn't been labeled. It had a sharp, hooked beak between deep eye sockets. I stuck my finger through to the back of the skull.

I sensed rather than heard Peter enter the room. When I turned I saw he was wearing a blue jacket with white pinstripes, a crisp white shirt, a navy tie with white flowers, and blue slacks. His shoes were shined.

"You dressed up," I said.

"It's not every day I have a brunch date."

"This isn't a date, Peter."

"It's a barn owl," he said, pointing to the skull. "Look at the sockets, how they sit on the side of its face. Compare it to this one." He drew close and picked up the squirrel skull. He was wearing cologne. "A squirrel can't see anything except what's right in front of him," he said. He held it up to my face to demonstrate; I looked through the empty sockets at him.

"I'm not here for a lesson," I said.

"I have the full skeleton," he said. "Complete owl. A rare find. Stay for breakfast."

"I'm not hungry."

A shriek came from the bathroom, then a loud thump. He set the squirrel skull back on the mantel in line with the rest and smiled.

"See, you've made the kestrel mad."

Peter turned and went back down the hall. I heard the bathroom door open and then click shut. In the kitchen, there was a full pot of coffee, and I could smell the yeast of fresh-baked bread.

---

I couldn't know this yet, but they would call it the fastest storm of the century. I was at the search and rescue station at the bottom of the canyon road waiting for rescue calls when the clouds locked in on the west side of the mountain and three inches of rain fell in a single hour. The river surged. When my cabin dislodged from the canyon wall and slid down the hill, the water was there to usher it through the town, past the fire station and the post office, past the elementary school with the giant wooden bear out front, and eventually down the mountain in pieces. And then it was done. The clouds moved out, and when the phone finally rang at the station, it was Peter calling to tell me that my cabin was gone. After spending those early morning hours balancing on the edge of the river, searching for my belongings, I realized that the thing I was looking for wasn't in the river at all.

---

I was downing a cup of coffee in the kitchen when Peter came in with a yellow dress in his hands. My yellow dress, with a silk ribbon that wrapped around the waist.

"I tried to get the stains out," he said. He rubbed at a small brown mark on the shoulder, then held the dress out to me. It had been ironed, careful creases down the sleeves. I could smell the detergent.

"Come on," he said. "You're soaked." He pushed it into my hands. "The bedroom is down the hall."

"I know where the bedroom is," I said.

He smiled as though my words meant more than they did, and I moved down the dark hallway. I locked the door behind me, tossed the dress on the edge of the bed, and started searching. My safe wasn't behind the stack of textbooks in the closet, or under Peter's dirty clothes in the corner of the room. But my shoes—the white ones with a small heel and yellow straps across the toes—those were under the bed.

I looked at the yellow dress. I didn't want to put it on, not at all. But it was dry and the mud on my pants was beginning to harden. I checked the lock on the door again and then unlaced my boots, took off my pants and my shirt, and pulled the dress over my head. It was soft against my skin, and although I hated to admit it, I was grateful he'd saved it. I considered putting my boots back on, but instead I took off my socks, slipped my cold feet into the sandals, fastened the buckles, and walked back down the hall.

"You found your shoes," Peter said. He was at the stove, pouring oatmeal into a pot of boiling water. "I collected what I could after the worst of the rain stopped." He pulled a loaf of bread from the oven. Smoke filled the room. I opened a window, and he waved a green dish towel at the air.

"That's mine," I said. "That dish towel."

He went to the stove, stirred the oatmeal, and turned the burner to low.

"She knows," he said. "Andrew's wife. She knows he's up to something. With someone. I heard her talking about it at work yesterday." He looked down at the pot of oatmeal rather than at me.

What I knew about Andrew's wife: her name was Ilana. She had an office on the second floor of Hughes Hall, a whiteboard on the door for messages. Her office hours were Mondays and Wednesdays from one o'clock to two o'clock. She didn't say her name on her voice mail recording but instead repeated her phone number. She drove a small silver hatchback with a dent on the back bumper. A collection of beaded necklaces dangled from the rearview mirror. I knew she went grocery shopping at the same time every Saturday morning and that she always ordered a cappuccino at the coffee shop on her way home. She pronounced *cappuccino* with an Italian accent. She didn't use sugar. She called the teenagers behind the counter *baristas* and liked it when they drew a leaf rather than a heart into the foam. They often made fun of her when she left. She was most beautiful with her hair down and a bold red lipstick on. She looked great in everything but orange.

Peter handed me a knife, and I sliced the burned bread.

Andrew and I had met two years earlier, when I got lost near the top of Devil's Backbone. I'd been up and down that stretch of the summit at least a dozen times, leading school groups and church groups, pointing out the high peaks of the Sierras to the north, Mojave Desert just barely visible to the east, and, on a clear day, the Pacific Ocean to the west. But none of those hikes had prepared me for that day in November when I was on my way down the trail alone for my final hike of the season, and I watched the clouds come in from the south and swallow up the mountain.

I could barely see the ground in front of me as I walked, but I took comfort in knowing my trail would hit the river in less than a mile and that all I needed to do was follow the water south to the parking lot. The clouds moved fast, carrying a light mist instead of rain. Twice they thinned enough that I could see Pine Peak off to my left, Iron Mountain at my back. Then the wind shifted and I was again inside a cloud, this one thicker and whiter. I checked my compass, which said I was walking west, but I was certain—absolutely sure—I was headed southeast, and I knew that up around that turn and down that ridge I would reach the river. I descended a rocky outcrop that was steeper than I remembered, and where I expected the trail to end, it continued. I stood for a long time at that spot, checking my map, my compass, waiting for the clouds to lift enough that I could see what was around me. But the world only grew whiter. That's when I started to run, certain I was hearing the sound of rushing water, confident it was this turn that would bring me to safety. Nearly twenty minutes later, when the trail finally ended, I walked out of the thick white cloud and into a grove of bare and burned trees. There was no river. No water at all. It was a classic case of bending the map.

And so I screamed my voice hoarse, and when the sky went dark and the wind picked up, I found a charred log and crawled inside to wait out the night. I fingered the flaking skin of the tree and listened to the blood in my ears, a weak pulse quickened only by the fear that I might die.

It was Andrew who pulled me out the next morning.

Months later, I drove to the search and rescue building to thank him, and on the map he showed me where I'd made a wrong turn, where I'd ended up, and the route they'd taken to find me. It was when he placed his finger on the exact point of rescue that he looked up and smiled, and the next day I bought a radio that allowed me to tap into local rescue activity and listen to their missions. I studied videos of airlifts—altitude sickness on Cucamonga Peak, open ankle fracture on Ice House Canyon Trail, hypothermia at Sunset Ridge. I collected newspaper articles about the lonely souls who had been stranded. I plotted rescue spots and filled in charts with personal information of those who had been lost and found—their genders and ages, their original destinations, and their rescue locations. I calculated survivability rates based on all these factors and mapped out where new lost subjects would likely be found given how much time had passed since they'd last been seen. I knew this mountain so well that when I finally begged Andrew to let me join the team, he agreed, even though he had a rule against it: never hire the rescued.

———

"Professor Connell!"

Peter replaced the lid on the oatmeal and went to the kitchen window.

"Professor Connell!"

A young woman with a high ponytail and running clothes stood at the bottom of his steps holding a large brown box.

"Be right down," Peter called. He pushed the wooden spoon into my hand. He held his hand over mine, and I pulled away. "Stir the oatmeal every minute or two, or it will stick to the bottom," he said.

I opened cabinets and cupboards. I looked under the kitchen sink, in the pantry, even in the junk drawer at the far end of the counter. And in each of these places, I found a tiny bit of my life. My broom. My dented saucepan, the handle newly glued and secure. My travel mug. My plaid washcloths, clean and folded into neat squares. Everything was in the exact drawer where it would have been in my own cabin. It wasn't just that Peter had found things in the river from the night before. I knew he'd been sneaking into my cabin when I wasn't there, taking things from my drawers, my cabinets. Small things at first. Spices. A dustpan. A few pieces of silverware. I knew he hoped I might come to him, ask him to return the things that had gone missing. Occasionally I'd walk across the road to his porch, not to ask for my things back, but to sit and drink coffee and pretend I didn't know what Peter was doing because I needed Andrew to think I was dating someone else. He once told me he couldn't leave his wife unless our betrayals were equal, unless I also had someone to leave. And one evening, when Andrew and I arrived at my cabin, I caught the lingering smell of Peter's cologne and saw something in Andrew shift, a hint of jealousy that made him stay longer, visit more often.

But I only slept with Peter once.

It was the day the boys went missing, when I had collected all the information we knew about them, compared it to other cases, plotted the graph, and calculated the numbers. When Andrew finally sent me home that night, I handed him a report with the three most likely places they'd find the boys based on their ages, the terrain, the weather, the elevation. I told him that if they made the rescue in under twenty-four hours, they would find the boys alive. They had been missing for just eight hours when I went home to bed, and deep in the night, when the skies above my cabin went silent, I knew the team had them. It was only when Andrew called to tell me that I'd been right about the location but wrong about their chances of survival that I walked across the road to Peter's cabin and Andrew drove home to his wife, both of us looking for someone to tell us we had done our best.

———

I heard Peter's voice at the door and closed the drawer of silverware I was staring into. The young woman followed him inside. Peter placed the box on a chair next to the row of skulls and started to empty it.

"We weren't sure you'd have power," she said, "so we only got you nonperishables."

She couldn't be older than twenty, and as he lifted out cans of corn, green beans, and chickpeas, she looked on, increasingly excited by each item. Energy bars, gummy bears, chocolate.

"So nice of you, Liza," Peter said.

"We went to the pet store in town to get a few treats for the kestrel."

"He's recovering well," Peter said. He pulled out a plastic bag and inspected it. Two suction-packed mice, their fur a shocking white, their pink tails intertwined. "But I suspect he'll need another week or so to heal completely."

"Seriously, Professor Connell, it's some kind of miracle you still have power." Liza looked around now, spotting me standing in the kitchen doorway with the wooden spoon in my hand.

"Oh, Mrs. Connell!" Liza said. She walked across the living room, her hand extended.

"I'm not—"

"Sit down, sit down. Both of you," Peter said.

He pulled three bowls from the cabinet as the girl went on and on about intruding on our morning.

"Don't be silly. We're happy to have you join us," Peter said.

She apologized again, but I could tell she wanted to stay. She arranged herself at the kitchen table, a napkin in her lap, her elbows propped on the rough wood. Peter set a bowl of oatmeal in front of her and pulled out a chair for me. He sprinkled walnuts into my bowl and then his, and when he handed Liza the bag I couldn't help but notice her disappointment. A cold breeze hit my legs, and I closed the window behind me.

"Yes," Peter said, "there's a chill in the air this morning. Excuse me for just a minute."

I'd never seen Liza or any other student climb the steps to his house. He never talked about his students, and I'd always assumed they didn't like him, that they tolerated him for an hour and a half twice a week and then went home. I nodded at Liza's outfit. "Did you run today?"

"No. We tried," she said. "A bunch of us from class. They said all proceeds would go to victims of the flood, but they were already at capacity. So we went to the grocery store instead." She grinned as though she were waiting for something. Applause, perhaps. Or a gold star. I smiled. Liza lifted a spoonful of oatmeal to her mouth, looked at me, and put her spoon down.

"No, no," I said, "go ahead, please. No need to wait."

"No, it's fine. Really, I don't mind."

I leaned out and peered down the hall. Liza did too, then smiled at me, at her oatmeal, around the room again, and back down the empty hall.

"Well, tell me then," I said. "What is he like as a teacher?"

"Oh, you know," Liza said.

"He doesn't talk much about the job."

"He's everyone's favorite. Students really respect him. Honestly, he makes me want to be an ornithologist."

I assumed Liza had an A-minus in his class and that she was angling for the solid A. I knew her type. I had been that type. I, too, would have sought out charity events, would have raised money for flood victims. But I never would have showed up at my professor's front door, not on a Saturday. And not alone.

"How did you know where we live?" I asked.

"Well," she said, "it's just that he talks about this place a lot."

I looked around the kitchen. "What does he say about it?"

"No, I mean he talks about what it's like to live up here. In the village. And your work too. He told us about that girl and her mother you found on Ice House Canyon Trail. And the guy with the broken ankle at Manker Flat."

"Toe."

"What?"

"He broke his toe. Made it all the way down the trail. I just drove him to his car."

"Oh. Still," she said. "It's really great what you do."

I wondered if Peter had told his students about the three boys, the ones I had been so wrong about. I searched her face for any sign of judgment or pity, but she looked away. I didn't know what that meant, so I picked up my spoon and ate my oatmeal.

Peter apologized as he came down the hall and into the kitchen, his voice echoing off the walls. "It just took me a while to find this," he said.

He was holding a sweater of mine, long and gray, with a patch on the elbow and buttons down the front. He draped it around my shoulders. I put my arms through, pulled it tight around my chest.

The sweater, I was sure, had come from the second drawer of his dresser. And I knew that if I opened the closet in the living room, I would find my snowshoes. That if I pulled out the bottom drawer of the built-in shelves near the fireplace, there would be a stack of my wool blankets. My carabiners and ropes would be on the floor in the hall closet. My windbreaker hanging above them. Then I pictured the bird in the bathroom, not perched on the shower rod or on the edge of the sink, but with his healthy leg tied down to my safe.

———

Bird shit was everywhere—on the safe, the floor, droppings marking the short range the leash offered. The bird flicked his tail, pumped his head up and down, and let out a high and rapid *Killy! Killy! Killy!* Wings wide, he lunged at me and shouted again. *Killy! Killy! Killy!*

Peter pushed by me, Liza right behind. They both kneeled in front of the kestrel and Peter put out his hand. The bird dropped its head into its shoulders, eyes full of fear. With tweezers, Peter snagged a stray piece of beef from the floor and held it close enough for the kestrel to reach.

*Killy, killy.*

Peter waited. Liza watched, a smile at the edge of her mouth. The bird looked up at us again, then stuck his neck out for the meat. One swift movement: lunge and swallow. The bird jumped to the top of the safe. Peter wrapped his hands around the animal's chest. "Behind the safe, Liza. The hood."

Liza found the small leather pouch and pulled it over the bird's head, cinching it tight around his neck.

"He won't hurt you," he told me.

Liza followed Peter out of the bathroom, and there I was, alone with the hooded bird. When I bent down, its chest feathers ballooned. I turned the dial to the left, right, and left again until the lock clicked open. The bird lifted a leg and spread its wings, then finally went quiet and still.

Inside the safe was my lease for a cabin that no longer existed. An unused checkbook, damp but not ruined. My social security card, faded and creased at the edges, barely even wet. A passport I'd used only once, when Andrew and I drove across the border into Mexico because I'd never been before and because he said everyone had to go at least once. It was the only trip we'd taken together, staying in Tijuana long enough for me to eat a mango on a stick and to see a donkey painted like a zebra. On the way back, somewhere between San Diego and Los Angeles, I realized he was married. It wasn't anything he said; he was careful that way. Rather, it was something about the way he kept checking his watch, glancing at the clock on the dashboard. He was rushing to be home in time for dinner.

I found eight hundred dollars in the safe and put it in the pocket of my sweater along with my passport and social security card. I thought it would feel better to have them. I was wrong.

At the back of the safe were some newspaper clippings. On top, a picture of the three boys in their basketball uniforms, celebrating a win with their teammates. I liked seeing the three of them together, arms in the air, mouths open, smiling—less than twenty-four hours before their hike. Stapled behind the picture were the obituaries, printed just days later. I folded the clippings into a square and dropped them in my pocket.

The last thing in the safe was a beaded necklace that

had once hung from Ilana's rearview mirror. I slipped it over my head and tucked it into the neck of my dress. This didn't make me feel better, either.

———

Down the hall, Peter was bent over a Tupperware container half full of bones. He was pulling them out one by one and handing them to Liza, who lined them up on the living room floor, ribs against the sternum, loose vertebrae above that.

"It's a full set," Peter said. "It shouldn't be too hard."

She sorted the claws. She named each bone—pelvis, femur, tibia, fibula—and arranged them into a neat leg. When she was done, Peter sent her to the mantel to retrieve the unlabeled skull.

"Scrub jay?" she said.

"No, look at the eyes," Peter said, taking the skull from her. "Look at where they are."

"Robin?"

"It's an owl," I said. "Barn owl."

They hadn't heard me enter the room. When they turned, they didn't look at my face or my sweater or even my pretty dress. Just at my hands. The hood was still fastened around the kestrel's neck. The rope, tied to his leg, swayed in front of me. I had expected a fight, but the kestrel had barely responded when I picked him up and carried him down the hall.

"Mrs. Connell?"

I noticed for the first time that Liza had the tiniest lisp, as though she couldn't quite get her tongue around the word *Mrs.*

"What are you doing?" Peter said, setting down the skull.

"I don't think you should hold him like that," Liza said. "It's better if you—"

I stepped toward them. I liked the weight of the bird in my hands. I felt important holding him, the way I often felt in the moments after finding someone huddled under a bush for protection from the sun or trapped at the bottom of a canyon.

"We should let the bird go, Peter," I said.

"He's not ready," Liza said. She had moved away, toward the coatrack, closer to the door, and I realized she was scared of me.

"He'll die," Peter said.

"You can't just tie him down like that."

"That's how they get better," he said.

"There isn't even a window in the bathroom," I said. "Will you help me, Liza?"

"I think—"

"It will only take a minute. We can just bring him up to the top of the canyon, put him near the—"

"I think maybe I should go," she said.

"Yes, of course," Peter said.

"It's just that I have this test to study for, and—"

"No need to explain," he said. "We've kept you long enough."

Liza retrieved her sweatshirt from the kitchen and came back without looking at me or the bird. Peter met her at the door.

"Thank you for the food, Liza," he said. "It was very kind of you."

"Bye, Liza," I said. "Good luck with your test."

She looked at Peter and then back at me. She waved and mumbled something. It might have been *goodbye*. Peter closed the door behind her.

"What are you thinking?" he said. He reached for the kestrel, and I pulled the bird into my chest.

"Don't squeeze it like that," he said. "Birds don't like that."

"Let it go," I said.

"I already told you—"

"Let it go, and I'll stay."

He kept coming at me.

"Did you hear me? I said I'll stay. For good. Let the bird go, and I'll stay here with you."

Peter stopped, lowered his hands. "Of course you'll stay," he said. "You have nowhere else to go."

———

I was certain that on this Sunday morning, just like every other Sunday morning, Andrew and his wife would play tennis on the clay courts near the community center at the base of the mountain. On their way home they would stop at the fruit stand on Second Street, where they would each order a fresh coconut. They'd eat it at the picnic table in the shade on the far end of the park, high above the Los Angeles Basin, in the shadow of the San Gabriel Mountains, and when they were done, they'd drive back to their two-bedroom bungalow on Eleventh Street, where they'd both shower. Not together.

Andrew would put on his uniform and tell Ilana he was on the overnight. He'd tell her to keep her fingers crossed that there were no fires or floods. He might even say he loved her. And then he'd drive up the mountain, park his car at the station, and walk to the end of the dirt road, where he'd see the empty canyon wall. He would feel bad for me, I knew that. But it wouldn't be enough for him to leave her.

———

Peter went to the kitchen and finished emptying the box of food Liza had brought. He tore off the flaps and put an old blanket in the bottom.

"This is the best we can do," he said, reaching for the bird. Again he held his hands over mine, and this time I let them linger for a moment.

*This could be okay*, I thought. It would only be for a few months. Six at the most. Peter would be easy enough to leave.

I set the chickpeas Liza had brought on the pantry shelf, where I always kept canned goods. The chocolate went into the drawer with the cookies and cakes. I dumped the leftover oatmeal into a Tupperware container and stuck it in the fridge on the second shelf, then scrubbed the pot, dried it, and put it in the cabinet under the microwave. I threw the gummy bears in the trash, put the coffee cups on the shelf next to my set of mixing bowls, and slid the spoons into the drawer next to the sink.

"Peter."

He turned to me.

"The wine opener goes over here." I opened the drawer next to the stove and showed him.

"Yes," he said, "I can never remember that one."

"And the sharp knives should all face the same direction."

"Of course," he said. "Actually, can you hand me one?"

He pulled the hood off the kestrel. The bird didn't call out or try to escape. He only shook out his wings before resting them on his back. Here, in the light from the window, I could see the bird's colors: his bright-orange chest, dotted with dark spots; his slate-gray wings, folded neatly across his back; a black streak, like wet mascara, running down from his eye. He was beautiful.

I handed Peter a knife. He held up the plastic bag and sliced it open, then shook one of the mice into the bottom of the box. The kestrel stepped on it, clutching it in his talons as I sat down and watched. He plucked at the white fur, teased away the skin, dug his beak deep into the hole he'd made. I could hear the announcer at the bottom of the canyon road calling out the names of the fastest runners as they crossed the finish line. The crowd was cheering. Someone had a cowbell. At the sound of an air horn, the kestrel lifted his head and looked toward the window. The feathers between his eyes were red with blood.

# SEA WOMEN

When the US Coast Guard calls that morning and plays the recording—a woman's voice screaming for help, screaming that her boat is sinking—Pam Everly knows it isn't her daughter. She knows, intellectually, that there is no way. Elsie is in Jeju, taking pictures of women in wet suits who are diving for—for what, Pam can't remember exactly. For animals? For shells? "For sea things," Pam tells the coast guard. But the man on the phone doesn't care what the women in South Korea dive for. He cares whether it is possible that Elsie might be on a boat in Boston Harbor. So he plays the recording again, explaining that the call has come from the cell phone in her daughter's name—*yes, he is sure*—and he asks Pam to listen. Listen carefully.

Pam can remember the exact pitch of Elsie's infant wail, the piercing screech of her toddler years. But she has never heard her grown daughter scream, has no idea what those sounds might grow into, how they might mature in a woman's body. "Again," she says. And the man on the other end plays it, and Pam searches in this frantic voice, this voice that could be her daughter's—her Elsie—for anything that sounds familiar. It is after the third time she listens to the recording that she is convinced this isn't Elsie, but she tells the nice man, "Well, maybe. It might be," even though she is certain. Just in case.

Their last phone conversation, three weeks ago now: Pam, rushing to get out of the house and to the salon, slipping her black boots over her black jeans, brushing the lint off her black shirt, asking, "Why don't you quit this thing, Elsie? Come home early?" and before she had even a second to correct herself, Elsie already saying, "Job, Mother, not thing." And Pam, surprised not by the tone—she had had years to adjust to that—but by the word *mother*, that aggressively impersonal word, a new development. "Only you're not getting paid, not really," Pam said, pulling on her coat, and she knew as the mom—as the goddamn *mother* in the conversation—she shouldn't have said that, but by then it was too late, and by then Elsie was saying, "Mother, stop. Listen, I am getting paid," and Pam snapped back, "Free housing doesn't count."

When Elsie first got to Jeju, she sent long emails about the women she was supposed to photograph. They wouldn't let Elsie near them. They put their hands in front of the camera. They threw things at her when she tried to get on the boat with them. Elsie called every night that first week, and when Pam heard the shaking in her daughter's voice, she felt both terrified and relieved. She didn't want Elsie to be upset, and she wanted those women to trust her daughter. But Pam was glad her daughter still needed her. Thousands of miles away Elsie still needed her.

So she knows Elsie is in Jeju, that whoever is in Boston Harbor is not her daughter, but she is unnerved by the coast guard's call, and it has been three weeks since they have spoken—three weeks since Pam belittled her free housing—and so Pam picks up the phone. She dials her daughter's number, knowing Elsie will be sleeping, that her phone will be beside her bed, on silent, that it will go straight to voice mail.

"Hey, you've reached El. Leave a message."

This also is new, the shortening of her name, a nickname at twenty-two.

"I know it's late there, Elsie. You're probably sleeping. But just checking in. Give me a call, okay? When you've got a minute?"

Pam puts the phone down, further relieved after hearing Elsie's soft voice, nothing like the one on the recording. Nothing at all. That voice was deeper and louder, and Pam thinks now she might have heard, between the urgency and the fear, a hint of an accent. Southern, maybe. Anyway, Elsie would have told her if she was flying back to Boston, coming home two weeks early. A trip that big, that long. Certainly her daughter would have told her that. And yet. There had been other trips. Elsie always mentioned them in passing, months after the fact. Weekend escapes with her college friends and a boy Pam has never met. About the trips, Pam was always sure to sound happy for her daughter, but the news would send her into a spiral after the fact. She would get into bed late at night, her body heavy with exhaustion from standing all day, from a half dozen haircuts, a blowout, a color, an updo for prom. When she closed her eyes, she felt like she was still on her feet, so she stared into the darkness, wondering whose hair she had cut the day her daughter was at a protest in Philadelphia. A play in New York. A parade in New Orleans.

Pam has seen those pictures. Just once, when Elsie left her computer open on the kitchen table while she took a shower. Pam almost didn't recognize her daughter with all the glitter around her eyes, the tight purple dress, the sparkly beads dangling from her neck, and her hair—normally so wild and curly—straightened and tamed, falling neatly to her shoulders, held in place, Pam was sure, with expensive products. Pam scrolled through those pictures until she heard the water turn off, and then she retreated to the living room and sat on the couch, pretending to read the newspaper.

It is relevant, isn't it, for the coast guard to know that sometimes her daughter leaves without telling her? That she occasionally goes on extravagant adventures and ends up in New Orleans with gaudy beads around her neck? That she might have, this one time, taken Pam's advice, quit her job, and come home early?

She calls the man; he picks up after only one ring.

"Sometimes she takes trips," Pam says, and as she speaks—as she hears her *own* voice—she is suddenly uncertain about everything. The voice on the recording. The accent she thinks she might have heard.

"Ma'am?" the man says.

Pam looks at the clock. It has been only fifteen minutes since they hung up.

"Elsie," Pam says. "She's supposed to be in Jeju, taking pictures of those women. But sometimes—" Pam pauses, collects herself, clears her throat. "Sometimes she goes places without me knowing."

"Listen, we've got a boat out there now, and we're talking with the cell phone company," the man says. "So just sit tight, okay?"

She can hear in his voice that he is annoyed, but Pam doesn't apologize for wasting his time, for being a burden, a distraction. Because when Elsie moved home after college, Pam told her daughter she was sorry the job market was so bad. And that she was sorry for hovering. Sorry for her own busy schedule, the long days at the salon that she couldn't get out of—*the holiday season and all, everyone wanting to look nice for the family portraits, and all these winter weddings. Can you even believe it? Weddings in December?* Elsie didn't answer the question. Instead, what Elsie said was, "It's a fault, Mom. Apologizing so much." She said it was a sign of weakness, that women must stop doing that if they ever want to be taken seriously. Pam promised Elsie she would work on it, and she has been. It's the only reason she hasn't emailed her daughter to say she is sorry, to say free housing is a good start.

*Sit tight.* Pam knows what he means. He means, *stay calm, be reasonable.* She knows the reasonable thing to do is to go take a shower, to put on her black jeans and black T-shirt, dry her hair, put on her makeup, and go to work, where she has a full day of clients waiting for her. She checks her schedule.

Sylvia Guyette, whose son is allergic to peanuts and whose dog is allergic to protein, scheduled for a cut and color at ten.

Noah Clark, who, each time he sits in her chair, claims he has never once colored his hair—a fact Pam knows to be untrue. Lunchtime trim.

Rosa Waxman. When she called the week before, she requested the last appointment of the day. *A change*, she said on the phone. *Something big. A pixie cut. A bob, maybe?* Pam knew then that Rosa's affair was over.

Yes, Pam should do the reasonable thing. She should go to work, tend to her clients, their hair, their stories. Instead, she stands, retrieves the scissors from the drawer in the kitchen, and goes to her daughter's bedroom, where a stack of boxes lines the far wall.

A year ago, when Elsie first moved home from college, they'd fought about these boxes. Pam had only tried to be helpful, had thought it might be a nice gesture to surprise her daughter one night after Elsie went to see a movie alone. Pam unpacked her daughter's art books, lined them up on top of Elsie's childhood dresser. She stacked the binders and notebooks on the empty desk where Elsie used to study in high school. Just as she lifted some photo albums from the box, Elsie returned—the movie sold out—and stood in the doorway of her bedroom, indignant, her eyes and mouth open wide. And then Elsie stormed around the room, collecting the books and binders, ripping the photo albums from Pam's hands, shouting about betrayals and privacy and trust. Pam had never seen her daughter like this, and she watched as Elsie crammed all her belongings back in the box and shoved the box against the wall. Elsie stood with her arms crossed in front of her, shifting her weight from one leg to the other, not looking at Pam but eyeing every box in the room, like she was counting them. Pam thought, *My god. My daughter is hiding something.*

Pam hesitates as she stands in front of that wall of boxes. She knows she shouldn't go looking through her daughter's things. But this is different, she tells herself. She takes one of the boxes down from the high, orderly pile and slices the tape with the scissors, pulling open the flaps.

Yes, this is different.

She is only looking for phone numbers because she isn't sure now about that accent she thought she heard. And she isn't sure her daughter would tell her—her own *mother*—if she was coming home from Jeju two weeks early. She *is* sure, however, that she would have told one of her college roommates—Chelsea, Libby, or Dana. And so Pam is searching for something—anything—that might contain their phone numbers.

Box after box Pam searches, and, even though she knows she is alone, Pam can't shake the feeling that she is being watched because on the other side of the room, covering an entire wall, Elsie has hung the portraits from her senior art show, the only items she unpacked when she moved home. There is a close-up of a woman's mouth, her lips bright red, her teeth sinking into the flesh of a peach, a stream of juice dripping down her chin. Beside that picture, a close-up of a man's face. Shocking green eyes. Dark-brown hair. His mouth open, ready for the forkful of spaghetti. His beard covered in marinara sauce. A child with chocolate cake smeared down his cheek, onto his neck, his entire hand shoved in his mouth. Over a dozen images just like this, of filthy faces.

The night of Elsie's senior art show, the day before graduation, Pam walked around the gallery, taking in the other students' work—the portraits of grandparents, landscapes of Ireland, a black-and-white series of musicians posing with their instruments. She remarked to her daughter how beautiful they were, and her daughter seemed surprised—"They're okay, I guess"—and when they got to Elsie's series, Pam remembered thinking they were childish, vulgar, almost indecent. Pam was shocked, later that night, when the woman at the podium—some famous artist she had never heard of before—announced to a room full of proud parents and graduates that the department's most prestigious award would go to Elsie Everly for her stunning series, *Still Life: Family Dinner.*

As the show closed down and people cleared out of the gallery, Pam stood once more in front of her daughter's photographs, staring at the woman, the peach, the stream of juice running down her chin. Pam shoved her hands deep in the pockets of her coat, fighting the sudden urge to wipe it away, to clean that girl up. There in her daughter's bedroom, emptying the contents of each box out on the floor, sifting through Elsie's belongings, digging through her secrets—thirty minutes passing, then an hour, and another—Pam looks up at the picture again and is surprised to find that urge is gone.

———

Far from Elsie's bedroom, the phone rings, and Pam stands up, leaving the boxes open, running down the stairs, through the living room and dining room to the kitchen. She will tell the coast guard to play it for her again, one more time, and she will listen more closely, more carefully to the voice on the recording. She won't let him say no. She will refuse when he tells her to sit tight. She lifts the phone to her ear.

"Hi. It's me."

This voice. Not the coast guard's voice. Not a man's voice at all.

"Elsie?"

"You won't believe this. These women, my god! Grandmothers, all of them. Up and down, over a hundred times a day."

And now Pam is sure the woman on the recording, the one screaming for help, had a voice nothing like Elsie's. This voice—her daughter's voice—is higher in pitch and sounds so far away.

"Elsie, where are you?"

"I was out with them all day. They finally let me on the boat. These women. Just goggles, two flippers, and a belt of weights around their waists. When they surface, their lungs whistle. They invited me for dinner. You won't even believe the shots I got."

"You haven't called," Pam says. "You haven't called in three weeks." And now she is weeping, openly and without reserve. She covers her mouth to stifle it. Her daughter doesn't apologize.

All she says is, "Mom, are you listening to me?"

---

It will take Pam years to perfect the telling of this story, years before she knows exactly when to pause, when to slow down, when to speed up. Only once does she add a little flourish, an unnecessary exaggeration she later regrets, extending the length of time Elsie was missing. It is a betrayal of the facts, and she believes facts are important, and the truth is that for an excruciating three hours, she was forced to imagine her daughter at the bottom of an ocean, her hair wrapped around her face, tight around her neck, strangling her. To lie, to say it was a full day—well that, she thinks, is cheap, and she vows never to lie about it again.

What the young women in her chair always ask:

*Who was it then, out there screaming? If it wasn't Elsie?*

The question haunted Pam, too. Because she doesn't know, and no matter how many times she called the coast guard, all he would say was that there had been some confusion, some unfortunate miscommunication at the station, and he couldn't say anything more than that. She stewed, remembering his ridiculous confidence when he first called, his certainty that the voice was coming from Elsie's phone. So she called again, this time calibrating her tone, steadying her voice, and she told the man that he had been careless, that he couldn't possibly understand the damage he had done. Pam could sense, on the other end of the phone—through the silence, through his breath alone—a mocking smile, a self-assured smirk. "I'm sorry you feel that way," he said. It wasn't an apology. It wasn't even close.

The men in her chair always want to know where Elsie is now, and Pam tells them, but she knows she is a step or two behind. She tells one man that her daughter is in California, taking pictures of the wildfires, but finds out later Elsie has already moved on to Seattle to document the whales. She tells another man Elsie is with the whales, and then discovers she is actually in Florida for Hurricane Matthew.

It is the mothers who always ask about the boxes.

*What did you find in them? What had she been hiding in there?*

Maybe they really want to know Elsie's secrets. Maybe they are truly interested in what it was her daughter kept in those boxes. Pam doesn't tell them. It is already enough— too much, indeed—that Pam uses this story to entertain. But Pam doesn't think these women really want to know anyway. They are looking for something else. Permission, perhaps. Her blessing, maybe. Reassurance that everything will turn out okay if they open those boxes in the base- ment—the ones their daughters left behind—and examine every secret they refused to unpack.

# SHOVELBUMS

MIKE GREW UP in Florida, worked at a meatpacking plant in Chicago for two years, quit that job, moved west, and started shovelbumming when he was twenty-two. At fifty-six he was terrified of the apocalypse and training his body to survive without electricity. He bought a rotisserie chicken each week, stored it in a dresser drawer in his motel, and ate a little from it each night. He believed whoever could survive the apocalypse would get to repopulate the earth.

Brooke laughed because she thought Mike was joking, but then he unwrapped a plastic bag and showed her his chicken carcass. She thought that was disgusting but didn't say so because this was her first summer as a shovelbum and she'd only just met Mike three hours before. Instead she talked about the success of her master's thesis and the new Platypus hydration system she was looking forward to carrying on their first job.

Calvin had a PhD that Mike distrusted and Brooke envied. He specialized in Iron Age archaeology, spoke three languages and read six. But he still couldn't find a full-time job. Even in the desert, even in June, he never carried water or food. Just a two-liter bottle of orange Fanta. He didn't mind if it got hot or flat.

Trina, the crew chief, picked them up at the Salt Lake City airport. She told them that she'd arrived thirty minutes early and that this was something they should get used to. She said breaks were never a second longer than fifteen minutes and lunches were exactly half an hour.

Together they moved from one job to another—never staying in a place longer than ten days, always sleeping in motels along the way—evaluating potential sites and updating existing ones for the National Register of Historic Places.

## CLIFF DWELLINGS

Deep in the Wasatch Range, three miles down a two-track road, past an old ranch, beyond an airway beacon, and through a dried-out ravine, they surveyed a string of wide-mouthed caves in the steep limestone cliffs. They found one unnatural rock alignment and a heap of dead bats. Trina filled out the inspection papers. They moved south.

They updated site records at Butler Wash—new pictures, new coordinates. They noted ground disturbances caused by erosion, graffiti on the east wall, and evidence of a party. Wine coolers, cigarette butts, Doritos.

Next, they surveyed Mule Canyon, Fry Canyon, Mesa Verde.

## CHACOAN GREAT HOUSE

The site inspection of Una Vida was delayed first on account of a monsoon and second on account of the stomach flu. When they finally reached the site four days late—all a few pounds lighter and a little gray— the inspection was delayed for a third time on account of ants. Enormous, pissed-off ants with black bodies and red asses that swarmed up their trowels, over their hands, under their shirts, into their pant legs.

## HOME-COOKED MEALS

Brooke bought a toaster oven for her motel room. On Sundays she baked a week's worth of sunrise muffins from scratch and warmed one each morning for breakfast. At night she baked casseroles and wandered the motel hallways looking for someone to share her food with because she hated to eat alone.

## SHIT LIST

"Catclaw acacia," Trina said.

"Locusts," Mike said.

"Scrub oak," said Calvin.

"No, wait," said Mike. "Barrel cactus."

"Oh," said Trina. "I second that."

"What about the prickly pear?" Brooke asked. "The ocotillo? The jumping cholla?"

"Those fuckers," Mike said.

## JOSHUA TREE NATIONAL PARK

A hundred and fifty miles east of Los Angeles, deep in the desert, they parked at the beginning of a washed-out road, walked seven miles, stopped for lunch in the shade of a creosote bush, walked for another three to a dried-out dam, and found nothing more than trash: fence staples, light bulb fragments, crushed aluminum cans, nails, hinges, a metal spoon, a tobacco tin, a clear glass bottle, balancing weights for a car wheel. The only item that could be dated was a single bullet casing from 1867. But even that was misleading. It was a leftover from a television shoot. *The Magical World of Disney*, circa 1961. The episode: "Chico, the Misunderstood Coyote."

They were supposed to be looking for petroglyphs, but what they really wanted to see was an oasis, a mirage, a conspiracy of the eyes, an optic error—something to call home about. They stared hard at the heat rising in waves off the desert floor. They wanted skeletons to appear amid dust storms, the distant mountain range to vanish. They tried hard to hallucinate something interesting, and when nothing appeared they made it up.

Mike said the rock mounds looked like the pregnant bellies of giant women, all of them out there on their backs, waiting for him to return to them.

Brooke thought the Joshua trees looked like angry men with spiky fingers pointing down at them, scolding them for coming out this far. Calvin disagreed. He thought they looked more like cheerleaders. Arms out wide, pom-poms in hand—an entire desert of trees cheering for them, all the way back to the Jeep.

Trina didn't know about the rock mounds or the trees, but she thought the tarantulas just looked like tarantulas, especially at sundown, when they crossed the road looking for mates. She ran over them whenever she could, even though the road signs said not to.

## ATTIRE

Only once, on their first day in Yuma, did Brooke wear her hair in pigtails under her wide-brimmed hat. When they gathered at the Jeep in the dark of the morning, Trina told her to take them out. Pigtails, she said, were Mike's favorite.

Mike's other favorite was his Grateful Dead T-shirt, the one with the hole across the back that measured ten and a half inches in diameter. When he bent over to inspect a surface deposit, fibers split, and the hole opened wider. By lunch he had a sunburn in the shape of a circle. He asked Brooke to help him moisturize it with lotion. She said no.

Brooke also said no when Trina asked her if she had duct tape in her pack. When Brooke asked why she needed it, Trina lifted her left foot, and a thin stream of yellow sand fell to the desert floor. She had a hole the size of a nickel in the sole of her boot. With a little tape, she thought they might last through the season.

To everyone's surprise, it was Calvin who had remembered the tape, and he helped Trina with her boot, even though she told him he was doing it all wrong.


## YUMA, ARIZONA

In the far corner of the desert, south of the Barry M. Goldwater Air Force Range, deep in the Cabeza Prieta National Wildlife Refuge, eleven miles from the border, they found a Bible, a tube of lip balm, and footprints. This wasn't what they were looking for.

They followed the footprints ten meters east and found a purple sweatshirt and an empty water bottle. Thirty meters north, under a creosote bush, stuck on a low branch, Brooke found a piece of paper. It was a drawing, in crayon. A yellow sun in the top corner. Three stick figures hovering near the bottom of the page. A man in a hat and sunglasses. A little girl in a purple dress. A woman in a matching green tank top and shorts. Their legs were too short and their arms were too long, but they were all holding hands.

Brooke tucked the drawing into her pocket and stood up. "We have to find them."

"There's more," Calvin said. "Look."

He had a woman's shoe, a pair of dirty socks, and a child's headband with three lace flowers covered in dust.

"They must be headed to Yuma," Brooke said.

"Or Dateland," Calvin said.

"Gila Bend, maybe," said Mike.

"We'll never find them," said Trina.

"But we have to try," Brooke said.

They all looked at Trina.

"Twenty minutes. And stay in the site bounds," she said.

Brooke walked west, Calvin east, Trina north, and Mike south. They met twenty minutes later, and no one found anything worth mentioning.

They left what they could, for others. Brooke left her trail mix, her hat, and the water pouch of her hydration system. Calvin left his half-finished bottle of Fanta. Trina left her jar of peanut butter, the rest of her bread. Mike left messages of encouragement in the sand. *Good luck. Be safe. Keep west.*

## YUMA, PART II

Brooke said she hadn't been able to sleep. She watched the news all night and checked the papers, hoping to find something about the missing family.

"Nothing," she said. "Can you believe it?"

"Really?" Calvin said. "You're surprised?"

Trina got in the Jeep. The others followed.

## ARTIFACT SCATTER

"Trina, I think I found something over here," Calvin said. "I think it's a tool," he added. "I think it's made from jasper. I think it's ancient."

Calvin was always right, which made his uncertainty all the more irritating, and on most days Trina told him to shut up, to let them just work in silence. But today she didn't say anything and neither did Brooke or Mike. Today, they hoped Calvin wouldn't stop because they didn't want to hear the wind or birds or coyotes. They didn't want to think about how thoroughly the sun was burning the skin on the backs of their necks. Or how the heat left their throats dry. Today they were happy to hear a human voice.

"I think there are more," he said. "Yes. Here. Look."

## YUMA, PART III

Brooke said she was going back. Trina said it was her day off—she could do whatever she liked. Calvin and Mike only went with her because they couldn't bear the thought of sitting in the motel all day.

They drove down the road as far as they could and walked the rest of the way. Brooke's hat was gone. As were Mike's messages, Calvin's Fanta, the bread, and the peanut butter. They stood together looking out across the creosote flats, and Brooke sensed movement happening all around them. She kneeled down and picked up a small stone. She rubbed it between her fingers, put it back down. She found another and placed it beside the first. She found more and balanced one on top of another.

Calvin and Mike joined her. They worked quietly, stacking the rocks, listening to the distant thunder of military planes. It took them nearly an hour to get it right, but in the end Brooke was satisfied. Three cairns, to show them the way.

### PER DIEM

The company gave them each sixty-three dollars a day for food and lodging. A night at the Frontier Motel in Yuma cost forty-five dollars and included a free continental breakfast. For dinner, they went to Low Country Restaurant and Saloon, beside their motel. By the time Brooke, Mike, and Calvin showed up, Trina was already there, flipping through the local newspaper, pretending she wasn't waiting for them.

"Anything?" Brooke said, pointing to the paper, "about the family?"

"What family?" Trina asked.

Brooke didn't feel like baking anything that night, so she bought a salad she shared with Calvin, a burger she shared with Trina, a plate of fries she shared with Mike, and a piece of chocolate cake she shared with all of them. Mike spent the rest of his per diem on beer. Calvin and Trina didn't buy anything because Calvin was saving his money for a ticket back to South Carolina, where he'd be living with his parents unless he could find a teaching job in the fall. Trina was saving her money to send to her daughter in Pittsburgh, for rent.

"You never told us you had a daughter," Calvin said.

"You never asked," she said.


## FAMILY

Trina had a son too. Although both children were grown, neither had a full-time job, and so they shared Trina's apartment while she worked out West in the summers. In the winters they all lived in the apartment together, even though it had just one bedroom and the toilet was unreliable.

Mike had a brother in upstate New York and a sister in New York City. He hadn't seen them in fifteen years because he once read an article that said the East Coast would be drowned in a tsunami event, and that prediction had kept him west of the Mississippi ever since.

Brooke was an only child and had recently started to resent her parents for not giving her a sibling because her mother was sick, and soon Brooke would have to return home to help take care of her.

Calvin was also an only child but never resented his parents because they'd lost two children before he was born.

## DREAMS

"I walked so far," Brooke said, "that I discovered a new flower. Red petals. Yellow center. I bent down. Put my lips to it. Extracted the nectar. Walked two thousand miles home with a mouth full of sugar, only to find my mother alone on the back porch of my childhood home. I put my lips to her spine and just like that her pain was gone, and every bad cell in her bones disappeared. Her skin turned from gray to pink and she opened her eyes and looked at me, and although I sensed her relief, she didn't go on living but instead began to dissolve right in front of me. Just turned to sand."

Mike drove the Jeep faster, said that was really sad. Calvin and Trina didn't say anything. Brooke wished she had different stories to tell.


## YUMA, PART IV

Mike ordered ten hamburgers from the dollar menu, ate one, and put the rest in the glove compartment. They walked four miles and stopped only once, to inspect an old railroad track.

Trina cut lunch short by five minutes because Mike was late getting to the Jeep that morning, and she walked nearly half a mile in front of the group for the rest of the day. When they caught up to Trina she was sitting on a rock, boots off.

"Blisters," she said.

"Heels or toes?" Brooke asked.

"Inside of my thighs. They popped when I sat down."

She emptied her boots of sand and laced them up tight, a puff of yellow pollen springing from her laces. She walked alongside the group for the last two miles, never complaining about the seams that were scraping her legs raw.

That night there was news of bodies on page twenty-three of the newspaper. Not out by the military base but further south. And not a family of three, but two teenage boys.

"It's like they want them to do it," Brooke said. "To cross here. Let the desert do the dirty work."


## YUMA, PART V

They met at the Jeep. No one said *Good morning* or *How are you?* or *How'd you sleep?* or *How long will we be out?* or *How many miles today?* Brooke didn't have muffins for any of them, and she didn't tell them about her dreams. They just stared at each other in the dim light of the pink neon motel sign. Trina took out the inspection papers. She tipped them toward the light. She said she would take care of it, and they all knew she'd falsify the report. They went back to their rooms. They shut their doors. They slept.


## LEFTOVERS

Mike woke up at noon, hungry, and remembered the burgers he'd bought the day before. He went to the Jeep, checked the glove compartment. His burgers were gone. He knocked on the door to Trina's room and told her they'd been robbed. Trina said it was unsanitary. He said he wanted his burgers back. She said they were in the trash bin behind the motel. He only found eight.

He knocked on Brooke's door to see if she was hungry, but she didn't answer.

He knocked on Calvin's door, and he did answer. Brooke was sitting on the bed, her shoes still on, her hands tucked in the sleeves of her shirt. She had been crying. Mike left them two hamburgers and went to his room, where he ate alone.

## LOW COUNTRY RESTAURANT AND SALOON

No one was hungry for dinner but they went anyway, and Trina told them they were already six days behind schedule and should be ready to move on in the morning. She didn't mention the missing family, but she did buy three rounds of margaritas, and that felt to Brooke like some kind of apology.

## CHECKOUT

At five thirty in the morning, Brooke went to the front desk. She showed the woman behind the counter the forty-three bites on the back of her right leg. She counted them twice, pointing at each red bump. The woman said her beds were clean. Brooke demanded a refund. The woman said there was no such thing. Brooke said she wanted to talk to the manager. The woman said she was it. The employee. The employer. The manager. The owner. Everything. And they didn't do refunds.

At the truck, Brooke showed the crew. She said they itched like hell. Calvin said not to scratch them, it would only make them worse. Mike said he would rub some cream on her leg if she wanted.

"Get in the Jeep," said Trina. "We're already late."


## FLAGSTAFF

They spent the first half of the day in the forest near Flagstaff, recording trees that had once been used as lookout towers, and the second half back at the Econo Lodge, searching their bodies for ticks. Brooke found two on her right ankle and one on her hip. Calvin offered to check her scalp, and Brooke said okay. She flipped her head forward and Calvin ran his fingers through her hair, behind her ears, across the back of her neck. He found one tick and a small twig. He crushed the tick between his fingernails. She offered to return the favor, but Calvin said Mike had already looked.

"You trust him?" she asked.

He bent his head. Brooke ran her hands around his neck and behind his ears. She took her time. She didn't find any ticks.

"I made cookies," she said. "They're from a box. But they're okay."

It was Brooke's grandmother who taught her how to bake, but Brooke lied and said she learned from watching cooking shows because she didn't want to talk about dead people. They ate four cookies each on the curb in front of the motel, and then Brooke took out the drawing. She unfolded it slowly. Stared at it for a long time.

"I think about her," Brooke said, pointing to the little girl.

Calvin looked at the picture and then looked away. "The cookies are good," he said.

## KEEPSAKE

The thirteen compartments in Brooke's backpack were intended to keep things organized. When they pulled out of the Salt Lake City airport three months before, she had two tubes of ChapStick in the top pouch, her emergency sunscreen in the left side pouch, and her tampons, pads, and ibuprofen in the second-smallest pouch on the front of the pack. She had two pencils and two pens secured in the slots intended for pencils and pens. Her map and compass were safely stored in the right pocket, which she could access without removing her backpack. Three months later, everything was thrown into the bottom of the pack. Everything except the crayon drawing, which she kept secure in the innermost pocket, the one with the zipper and the Velcro flap.

## WHITE STALLION INN

There was no continental breakfast, but the owner did provide a brown-bag lunch for $3.95—a turkey sandwich, an apple, peanut butter crackers, and a brownie. Lunch wasn't as advertised. They each got two slices of ham on white bread and a banana.

## SOME DESERT

They walked a sixteen-mile loop and didn't record or update a single historic site, but when no one was looking, Brooke carefully extracted a flower from the fishhook cactus and placed it in the pocket of her backpack. She knew it held no healing properties, that it couldn't cure her mother, but she liked the idea of drying it between the pages of her field guide and sending it to her from the next post office.

## SHIT LIST, CONTINUED

"Rattlesnakes," Mike said.

"I think desert centipedes are worse," Calvin said.

"Bark scorpions," said Brooke.

"The goddamn sun," Trina said.

## SOME OTHER DESERT

It was a creosote bush that punctured their two left tires, and it was only thanks to Trina that they carried two spares instead of one. Mike, Brooke, and Calvin were so grateful that they offered to change them, but when they couldn't figure out how to release the second spare tire from the hold under the Jeep, Trina told them to get out of the *fucking* way so she could *fucking* do it her *fucking* self. They all looked at each other. They laughed, Trina too, and then she said she was sorry but that it would be easier for her to do alone since the three of them were completely incompetent. She didn't apologize for that.

"I think we're all pretty tired of your insults," Calvin said.

"Well, I think we're all tired of the way you start every sentence with *I think*," she said.

Trina disappeared under the Jeep. Calvin looked hurt and then pissed, and he got down on his hands and knees and told Trina he thought she must be a terrible mother, treating people the way she did. Brooke and Mike escaped into a patch of shade at the front of the Jeep. Mike pulled a small black notebook out of his pack. He flipped to the back, wrote something. Brooke asked what he was doing. He showed her how he recorded every job he worked on and every person he worked with. He said it would serve as evidence when the entire world went to shit. Evidence of jobs he'd done, of women he'd known, and of miles he'd walked.

The petroglyphs in Danger Cave.

The lime kilns in Eureka.

The lighthouse in Tacoma.

"Got trench foot on that job. Slept in a tent instead of the motel because sleeping under a roof felt like cheating."

He started to take off his shoe to show her the scars. Brooke insisted he stop.

"How long will you do this?" she asked.

He shrugged. "I like it most days. Even days like this." He gestured to the back of the Jeep, where Calvin was still crouched, watching Trina work.

"I think you dropped a wheel nut, Trina," they heard him say. "I think you can get it yourself. I think you're the asshole."

Mike didn't ask Brooke how long she would do this because he knew it would be a minor miracle if she finished the season. She wasn't cut out for this kind of work. Most people weren't. He had a book full of names to prove it. People who wanted to think about these historic sites but not find them, or those who wanted to find them but not do the work to preserve them. People who wanted job security. Benefits. Regular hours. A house.

"Do you think they're okay?" Brooke asked. "That family? Do you think they made it?"

Mike shook his head. "I don't know," he said.

"Have you seen them before? Migrants, I mean. In the desert?"

He looked at her. "No," he said. "Never. They're doing their best not to be seen, Brooke. You understand that, right?"

She looked away, embarrassed. They were both quiet for a long time. Eventually Mike dropped his head and wrote something else in his book. Brooke asked if she could see.

"What are all the stars for?" she asked.

"My girlfriends," he said.

There was a star next to her name. There wasn't one next to Trina's.


**REGRETS**

Mike should have known it was Calvin who wouldn't make it to the end of the season, and Brooke should have known better than to cry about it, especially in front of Trina.

But Brooke thought she had a right to be mad. Because he left in the middle of the night. Because he told Mike about his new job but not her, and Mike couldn't even remember the name of the college, or what classes he'd be teaching, or whether it was a full-time position or part-time. Because Trina was the one he asked to bring him to the bus station. Because he hadn't left an address. Or email. Or phone number. No note. No goodbye.

On this last point Brooke was wrong, but she wouldn't realize it until almost two days later, when she undid the Velcro flap in her backpack, unzipped the innermost pouch, and found not just the picture and the crumbling cactus flower, which she'd forgotten to send her mother, but also a child's headband, still coated with a thin layer of dust.

## THE WOMAN IN WHITE

Mike wasn't sure what precisely was to blame for his food poisoning, but Brooke and Trina had a few guesses. All he wanted was to sit in the bathroom with his head against the cold wall while they inspected the stage station. Trina said she'd adjust his pay accordingly, and Mike said that seemed fair. Just one day. He'd be fine in the morning. He closed the door to his motel room, and Brooke followed Trina to the Jeep.

"He's faking," Trina said.

"I don't know. He looked a little yellow."

"He's scared of ghosts," she said. "This place is supposed to be haunted."

When they reached the site, they checked the structural integrity of the building and all the doors. Trina made notes of deterioration on the south-facing wall. They skipped inspection of the small graveyard at the back, so they had enough time to check the trails around the building before the sun set. They made it all the way back to the motel without Trina mentioning Calvin or how Brooke cried when she found out he'd left, and this made Brooke think that maybe Calvin was wrong, that maybe Trina wouldn't be such a bad mother.

## ANZA-BORREGO

On the first day of their final job, it snowed half an inch. They drove out to an old ranch, where the only structural feature still standing was the outhouse. Mike took measurements. Trina recorded them. Brooke made the to-scale drawing. They stopped at the SoCo gas station for dinner. Mike got three sausage biscuits left over from breakfast. He talked the cashier into giving them to him for half price. Trina got a piece of pizza. Brooke settled for a mini box of Frosted Flakes and a half pint of milk.

They drove through Galleta Meadows on their way back to the motel because Mike had heard rumors of a sculpture park. The rumors, it turned out, were true. Giant, rust-red metal statues scattered throughout the valley—dinosaurs, sea serpents, wild horses, mammoths, saber-toothed cats. Mike thought they'd return after the apocalypse. Trina thought that was an alarming thing for a scientist to believe. Brooke didn't say anything because everywhere she looked she saw the little girl. Behind the yucca. Under the sagebrush. In the shadow of a T. rex. A flash of purple. A bit of brown hair. But it was merely a trick of the light. Nothing there at all.

# FIXED BLADE

For my thirteenth birthday my mother promised to teach me how to shave my legs, but when I woke that morning it was my father knocking on my bedroom door. He stood waiting with his toolbox, a cooler, and a rusty coffee container filled with old nails. We needed to finish the roof of the Fullers' garage. My job was to hand him the nails so he could smash them into place.

I pulled on two pairs of pants and tucked them into my boots.

"A few solid hours should do it," my mother said to me. "Then we can take care of those legs."

She was squeezing her hands together the way she did when she'd had too much coffee and no breakfast. Every Friday, Ms. Beatty called me to the nurse's office at school and filled my backpack with two packets of instant oatmeal, two fruit cups, and four cans of soup. It was supposed to last through the weekend, but the food was always gone by Friday night. Even though I felt bad, I had started hiding a can of soup in my room when I got home from school.

"Budget cuts," I told my mother when she asked.

My father and I climbed into the truck, and my mother gave a weak wave from the window. But at the end of the dirt road, we turned right instead of left, and twenty minutes later my father pulled the truck onto the thick ice of Salem Lake. He tugged at the braid down my back.

130

"I'll make a man out of you yet," he said.

We drilled holes with his auger, hooked minnows to our lines, and dropped them into the water below. We sat out on the cold lake, waiting for the fish to fall for our tricks, and for every one caught, my father took a can of beer from the cooler.

"To make room," he said.

He pulled out his switchblade, opened the rainbow trout with a slice up the middle. The guts lodged between the blade and the handle, and he swore to himself as he untangled the mess. He slipped the trout into the water to wash it off and stacked it inside the cooler. Rainbow smelt, brook trout, yellow perch—none longer than six inches, and all of them barely worth keeping. We might have thrown them back, but I knew the stock in the freezer was low. I had heard my mother whispering about it earlier that week. When I reeled in our only bass of the day, my father handed me his fixed blade— his best knife, one he'd never let me use before, with a leather sheath, wooden handle, and long, thin edge. I held it to the fish's stomach.

"Lower," he said.

I moved the tip to the bottom of the belly, and when I stuck the blade in, a drop of blood slid down the white scales. The fish squirmed. I had thought it was dead.

"Keep going."

I unseamed the fish slowly, until the blade reached its mouth. When the fish stopped shivering in my hands, I pulled hard on the head like I'd seen my father do. It wouldn't budge.

"Put your thumb in there." He stood over me. My fingers were cold enough that I couldn't feel the inside of the fish, but I didn't like how it looked, my thumb lost in the fish's gaping mouth.

"Now pull hard," he said. I squatted over the dead fish. My legs shook. "That's right. Just like that." When the skin finally gave, I held up the string of guts, and my father gave a whoop. I tossed the guts on the ice and washed the fish in the lake water.

"Biggest one of the day," I said.

"Get all that black stuff out," he said. "No one wants that black stuff."

He was sitting on the lowered tailgate now, and even though the truck wasn't moving and the wind wasn't blowing hard, he swayed back and forth.

When we had eleven fish, he put the cooler in the bed of the truck and the keys in my hand.

"Happy birthday. You drive us home."

I pulled the bench seat all the way up, and although my foot barely touched the gas pedal, my father's bony knees banged against the glove compartment. The last can of beer was between his legs. He looked straight ahead, smiling at the windshield. It was on my twelfth birthday that he'd taught me to drive, but even a year later I sometimes mistook the brake for the clutch. The truck jerked forward to a stall. Beer sloshed out of the can onto his lap. He laughed loud enough to hurt my ears, and I did it again, this time on purpose, just to spill the beer. He raised the can and finished it with three big gulps.

"Smart-ass," he said. But he was still smiling, and I smiled back because I knew that was the best thing to do.

He slid open the rear window and threw the empty into the bed of the truck. The cans clinked against one another when I pulled off the ice and onto the road.

We were on Copper Creek Road when he fell asleep, his head against the window, his mouth open, his bottom lip pouty and wet. I imagined a hook through that lip, and then I imagined putting my thumb in there, pushing hard on the roof of his mouth.

When I took the turn onto Stevens Road too fast, my father fell into the middle of the seat. His head was on my lap, and I could smell the fish on his clothes.

I couldn't reach the gearshift, so I pushed in the clutch, moved the truck to the side of the road, unbuckled my seat belt, and turned off the engine. With my hands under his shoulder and my feet pressed low on the door, I pushed his body back up, then held him steady with my right hand while pulling the seat belt around him with my left. I clicked the belt into the buckle. His eyes opened. He smiled with half his mouth.

"I'm really proud of you," he said. He shook his head. "Fourteen, my goodness."

There was no point in correcting him. I put my own seat belt back on, started the truck, and eased up on the clutch so carefully the engine didn't even rev. He was asleep again before I pulled the truck into the ditch by the Fullers' driveway.

This was where I always left the truck when I didn't want Mr. Fuller to see my father. He was a nice enough man, giving my father a job in the middle of the winter, but he worked at the church in town, and he had certain ideas about drink and prayer. He sometimes gave us pamphlets about it at the end of a workday, and my father always made airplanes out of them and sailed them from the truck window. I walked up the long driveway with the can of nails in one arm and my father's toolbox in the other, but the Fullers weren't home anyway. I could tell because the only lights on were the two small lamps near the front door, the ones that were on timers. They clicked on every afternoon at three thirty, and I always watched them to see when our day was almost over. Today they reminded me of birthday candles.

Inside the garage, I looked at the graying sky through two big holes in the roof. I scattered a handful of nails around the floor and left two hammers and a handsaw near the ladder. With a dull pencil I found at the bottom of the toolbox, I scribbled a note on an old receipt, doing my best to make it look like my father's handwriting.

*Almost done. Will be back tomorrow to finish.*

I found electrical tape under the lacquer and the paint scraper, and I stuck the note to the front door of the house.

My father was still sleeping when I got back to the truck, so I drove to the end of the road and turned right toward town.

I left the truck in the back parking lot of Dottie's and hefted the cooler around to the front, where Dottie always let me sit. I pulled a cardboard sign from the side pocket of the cooler and waited for customers willing to pay a dollar for a fish. Men in overalls and heavy jackets went in and out of Hudson's Hardware, and women watched me from under hair dryers in the salon next door. But no one stopped.

As usual, it was Dottie who eventually came outside. "I'll take the biggest one you've got," she said.

I placed the bass in a plastic bag and threw in a few ice cubes from the cooler.

"Should stay cold for a few hours," I said. She handed me a dollar bill and took her fish inside. A black SUV pulled to a stop in front of the salon, and I knew from the license plate it was the Hayward family. Emily and Jack Hayward owned the salon, and their three daughters went to my school. The girls got highlights once a month and French manicures every two weeks. They each carried a tube of lipstick in the front pocket of their jeans. I packed up the cooler as fast as I could and slipped into Dottie's before they could see me.

Inside, I walked up and down the aisles until I found the section with toothpaste and Band-Aids. I scanned the shelves for a razor and picked a pink plastic one. At the counter, I handed Dottie back her dollar.

"Need fifty cents more, darling."

I waited to see if she might say something else. When she didn't, I looked her in the face because my mother said it was harder for people to say no that way.

"Need another fish?" I said.

She looked back at me. We'd played this game before.

"No," she said. I turned to put the razor back. "But I need someone to take the two boxes at the back of the store and stock those things on the shelves."

The toilet paper and paper towels were light, and even though the boxes were big, they emptied faster than the boxes with batteries or toothpaste. Dottie gave me the step stool so I could reach high enough to make the towers tall. Then she gave me the razor, and I put it in my jacket pocket.

I grabbed the cooler with the ten dead fish and stopped a final time at the shelf with the razors. I knew

I was supposed to use shaving cream, the way they did on commercials, but the smallest can said $2.49. I turned to see Dottie hunched over a mop and bucket. I'd done that job one day when we needed dish soap, and I knew it was hard, how you had to squeeze out all the dirty water before dragging the heavy strands of rope over the tiles. If I timed it right, she'd never see me slip the can into my pocket. But I couldn't do it. Not when she was a sure bet for a fish a week.

I walked back out to the truck. My father wasn't there. When I walked back around to the front, I could see Mrs. Hayward in the salon washing an old woman's hair, and Mr. Hudson's son, Ralph Jr., in the hardware store, counting money at the register. *So*, I thought, *he's back*. Ralph was old enough to be a high school graduate, but he had left our school and this town over two years ago. Everyone told stories about where he had gone and what he was doing. Some said he'd run off with a friend's girlfriend. Others said he was in the army, or a cult. Dottie told me she thought he was in jail. The worst of the stories obviously weren't true. He was alive, sitting in his father's warm shop, after all.

When Ralph first left, and Mr. Hudson went from house to house looking for him, I imagined scenarios where I found him. Sometimes he was in a city, working at a car dealership. Other times he was just a few towns over, working in his own hardware store where no one knew him. Most often I found him on a beach in Florida, hair dyed blond, eyes hiding behind sunglasses. In no scenario did I bring him back. Instead, I stayed with him, working where he worked. Sometimes we eventually got married.

I pulled the door open and went inside. The shop smelled of dust and mothballs. I walked up and down the aisles looking for my father, but by the time I got to the fertilizer and pesticides, I had already figured out he wasn't there. The wall near the register was covered with key chains. There was one with a purple rabbit's foot. Another with an American flag. I reached for one attached to a small snow globe, but before I pulled it off the hook I smelled the dead fish on my hands and stuffed my fists deep into my coat pockets.

"You looking for something particular?" Ralph asked. He was leaning forward, his elbows on his knees, clicking a pen.

"Just my dad," I said.

"We're fresh out of fathers. Expecting more the middle of next week." He put the pen between his teeth. I smiled at his joke.

"Maybe I could put one on layaway," I said. "Probably won't have the money by Wednesday."

"Don't do layaway here, sweetie. But for you we could probably make a deal."

"He would've been here in the last hour or so," I said.

"You check the back room?"

He pointed to the door at the back of the shop. A sign hanging on it said *Adults Only!* I shook my head.

"How old are you?" he asked.

"Sixteen."

He looked around the shop and then back at me. I gripped my fists in my pockets, cursing myself for not washing them at Dottie's.

"Well," he said, shrugging, "that's pretty close to eighteen." He nodded toward the closed door. "It's not locked. If he's not back there, I'm afraid you're out of luck."

The back room was bigger than the Fullers' garage, but all the empty boxes thrown in the corner and the makeshift aisles made it feel small, like our house. There was a case of glass pipes near the door, and the lock on the case indicated they were more valuable than the guns hanging on the wall behind them. Boxes of bullets filled the bins below the guns, and knives hung in neat rows further down the aisle. Fishing knives with wooden handles, hunting knives in leather sheaths, short blades for skinning, fixed blades with gut hooks, switchblades with smooth handles. I pulled one from a hook and scraped the tip against the corkboard. I added three more lines to spell out my initials and put the knife back.

On the far end was a rack of magazines I knew I wasn't supposed to look at. I'd seen magazines like this before, when boys would pass them around the school bus and dog-ear the pages they liked best. They looked at those pictures in a way they'd never look at me, and not just because those women were older or prettier or famous enough to be in magazines, but because they had enough money to buy new bathing suits for every pose.

I looked back at the door before lifting one of the magazines off the rack. The woman on the cover lay on her back, her hands cupped over her chest. One leg was bent to hide what should have been covered by underwear, and on her thigh, she had a mark the size of a thumbprint that could have been a birthmark or a bruise.

I brought the cover closer to my face and looked hard for any sign of a stray hair on her knee, the front of her shin, her ankle. But there was nothing. Just skin that looked polished and lacquered. I tore the cover from the rest of the magazine and folded it into a tight square. When I turned around, Ralph was standing there smiling at me.

"Not sure you'll find your father in those magazines," he said.

Here Ralph was in his flannel shirt and ripped jeans, not looking how I wanted him to look. I knew then he'd never been to Florida. He looked pale and sick. He looked wintered.

"He must be in the truck," I said.

I tried to leave. Ralph blocked the doorway. He pulled the magazine cover from my hand and unfolded it. I wished the rumors were true, that the worst had happened to him and that he was dead.

"She's all right," he said. He held the picture at arm's length. "But she has too much makeup around the eyes." He turned the image toward me. "Don't you think?"

I didn't look at the woman or at him. He slid the picture into my hand. His thumb brushed the inside of my wrist. He put his hand on my shoulder. I couldn't breathe.

"Go on, now," he said. "I've got to close up soon."

He patted my shoulder twice, and I crushed the picture in my fist until it was small enough to stuff in my pocket. Outside, Dottie's lights were off. The truck was still empty.

I stopped looking for my father. I didn't care how he got home.

———

Before I even entered the house, I could smell the dinner my mother had made, and I realized at that moment that I hadn't had breakfast or lunch. On each plate, there was a filleted and panfried fish, the last of what was in the freezer, I was sure of it. Mine was the one with the candle in it. She cut the one for my father in half and gave us each an extra piece.

"We'll finish the garage tomorrow," I said.

I handed her the cooler, and she put it on the counter. She lifted the cover. Although the fish were small, she looked relieved.

We sat down together, and she lit the candle. I knew better than to make a wish, but I paused long enough after she finished singing that she might think I had.

When I blew out the candle, all I could see in my mind were that woman's legs on the cover of the magazine. We ate in silence until she reached across the table and pushed my hair behind my ears.

"I swear you look older today. I swear it."

I didn't shrug her hand away because I knew she'd ask me what was wrong, and I didn't want to remind her of her promise. So instead I smiled and took another bite of fish.

"I am older," I said. "A day older than yesterday."

"You know what I mean. You look like a teenager."

"I am a teenager."

"Look at me." I didn't want to look at her. "Look at me," she said. "He'll be back. Don't you worry."

She tucked my hair behind my ear again, and I knew she hadn't seen anything new in me, only an old concern that wasn't even there anymore.

After dinner, she took the fish from the cooler and piled them in the sink. She washed them again, dried them with a paper towel, and pulled the cutting board out. She never said anything about the razor, and I didn't tell her I had one in my pocket. I went upstairs so she didn't have to explain why I didn't get a birthday present, and because I didn't think I could keep from crying if she tried.

I locked myself in the bathroom, took off both pairs of pants, and stared at my legs. The hair was thin and blond, but long enough to tug on. I unfolded the magazine cover and rested it against the back of the sink. Thick black lines ringed the woman's eyes. Silver glitter stretched across her eyelids to her temples. Her lashes nearly touched her brows. Ralph was right.

I didn't want my mother to know I was in the bathroom, so I left the water off and lifted my foot onto the closed toilet seat. I unwrapped the razor from its plastic bag and gripped it like a knife. That didn't feel right, so I flipped it around and held it between the pads of my fingers like a pencil. I dragged the dry blade up my shin and watched the thin hairs fall to the floor. I blew on the razor to remove the stray hairs and started again at my ankle. When the bottom half of my leg was clear, I straightened it and pulled the razor over my knee. Blood filled the creases in my kneecap, and when I bent my leg, the blood came faster. I pushed a wad of toilet paper on it and kept going, pulling long strokes up my dry thighs. Three hours in Dottie's store next week and I'd have enough money for the shaving cream.

When I was done, I compared my legs to the woman's in the picture. They were gray and flaky, and my thighs were covered in red bumps the woman's didn't have.

I opened the medicine cabinet and pushed aside the aspirin and eye drops. I finally found the bottle of lotion under the sink. It was nearly empty, so I took the cap off and stuck my finger in as far as I could. I scraped the sides of the bottle and smeared the lotion over my legs. They came alive with a sting that made me feel older.

Back in my bedroom, my legs bare and burning, I took out the last can of soup I'd hidden in my closet. I popped the top off, tipped it up like a drink, and tried not to listen for the click of the front door. But it was no use. I was still awake hours later, staring into the dark above my bed, when I heard him come in. I heard his heavy boots climb the stairs at an even pace, until they reached the top landing, where a loose board creaked in front of my door. When he knocked, I opened the door to him standing there, clothes reeking of fish. He held out a small paper bag. I opened it and saw something wrapped in an old towel. I reached inside.

"Careful," he said.

As I unwrapped the gift, he flipped the hall light on, and I pulled the leather sheath off the knife. The blade caught the light and flashed into my eyes. I squinted.

"You don't like it," he whispered.

It was just like his fixed blade but newer, sharper.

"I do," I said. "I do like it."

I ran my thumb across the edge, flipped the knife over, and stared down at the tag. I knew we didn't have that kind of money, had never had that much money at once. I knew that he'd stolen it, and I was glad.

# WHAT THE BIRDS KNEW

IN MY MOST vivid memory of my daughter, we are on the beach in Kauai and she is walking toward me, hair wet and tangled, legs pink with sunburn. Her purple bathing suit is too small for her. She extends her cupped hands toward me.

"Daddy, look," she says, opening her fingers. There in her palm, a turquoise egg, broken and empty. "Can I keep it?" she says, crawling onto the beach chair and into my lap. "Can we add it to your collection?"

Claudia is six, and this is the only trip I have ever taken alone with her. Before we flew here, the court decided she will live with her mother. I will see her every other weekend. We will split holidays.

My daughter hooks her feet around my calves, as if to hold on, and everything around me stops. How I will miss this gesture, the feel of her small toes on my legs, the weight of her in my lap. I put my nose to her head. I kiss that tangle of wet hair, taking in the smell of ocean and air and shampoo, and then I turn my attention to her hands.

"A myna egg," I say. "We already have one of these."

"But I like it," she says, shivering, and I wrap the white hotel towel around her.

"Okay," I tell her. "We'll bring it home with us."

She leans her head against my chest.

"Where did you find it?" I ask.

"Over there," she says, pointing at a mound of sand near the water.

I know then that this isn't a shell that has simply fallen from a tree, pushed out of a nest by a fledging bird. I know it was likely stolen out of some faraway nest by an eagle or a hawk, pierced open with a beak, left empty on the shore.

Claudia unwraps her feet from behind my legs and pulls them up into my lap. She puts the broken egg in the mesh nest meant to hold a drink, where I will forget it when we leave the beach that day. I wrap the towel tight around her, and I know that within a minute—maybe two—she will be asleep. And she is.

I have tried for many years to stop the memory here. I have tried to hold this moment in my mind, with Claudia asleep on my lap, folded up in my arms. I have willed her to keep sleeping, to pin her head against my chest, to never wake up or crawl down out of my lap. Sometimes I can make this part of the memory last for a few minutes. Sometimes I can suspend this moment for a few hours. But always, regardless of my efforts, Claudia wakes and pushes herself up on my lap, and I realize my shirt is soaked through with her sweat, her cheeks are red, her thin blond hair is stuck to the back of her neck, and when I put my hand to her forehead, I confirm what I already know: she has a fever.

The night we arrived in this little hotel, high up on a cliff on the west side of the island, I stared into the dark, counting Claudia's inhales and exhales, wanting more than anything to fall asleep to the sound of her breath. The longer I listened, the more unbearable it became. Finally, exhausted by the effort of trying to sleep, I got out of bed. I grabbed my sandals and a shirt from my suitcase, and I slipped out of the hotel room, careful not to let the door slam as I left. With my ear to the door, I listened to make sure she didn't wake up, and when I was certain she was still asleep, I went out to the garden and sat under the window of our room, waiting for my weariness to subside. I sat there for over an hour, listening to the night. This became somewhat of a ritual for me that week, sitting outside after she had gone to sleep, and sometimes I walked to the edge of the property where I could look down at the ocean, blacked out by the night, and I listened not to the sound of the waves pounding the rocks but to the terrible shriek of a bird I recognized, a scream meant to warn me that I had, without knowing it, come too close to a nest. I tried to find that nest in the daylight so I could avoid it, not wanting to bother the mating pair. But no matter how hard I looked, I couldn't see it anywhere on those cliffs.

———

It is on this trip I am supposed to tell Claudia that when we get home I will move out. I will take all my clothes and the few books I own, half the furniture, and the maple cabinet shoved into the corner of the small bedroom where a dresser should be, the one that holds my grandfather's egg collection. I will have to take it all away and move it into my new apartment, nearly an hour north, in Boston. I still haven't told her because I am worried she will be most upset about losing the eggs. She will no longer walk into the bedroom each morning, pull open those heavy maple drawers, and peer through the glass at a thousand shells, pinpricked and drained, stored and preserved.

All week I try. I really do. I start to explain it to her only to stop myself each time because I worry I will cry and I don't want to scare her. My silence keeps me awake, so on our last night I return to the garden and walk to the far end of the property, listening again for the bird. Alone and afraid about what the morning will bring, a return to a life that will be forever changed, I follow the sound back to the cliff. I lower myself over the edge, the ocean thrashing in the darkness below, my hands searching for a safe grip as I inch down to a slender platform of jutting rock. In the moonlight I can see the nest. I grip the rock hard with my right hand, lean into the wall of stone, reach out my left arm, and grab two eggs. Before I climb back up the steep cliff, I slip them into my jacket pocket. In the hotel, I study the eggs and confirm what seems impossible. It is the right season but entirely the wrong place. They shouldn't be breeding here. But in my hands are two eggs—brown and mottled, big enough to fill the cup of my hand. Peregrine falcon eggs.

———

When Claudia wakes up on our final morning, she still has a fever, and I am there in front of her, on my knees, placing a small velvet bag to her bare chest, securing it with an elastic bandage, wrapping it three times around her body.

"A magic pouch," I tell her, "to make you feel better faster."

When Claudia looks at me, her eyes vacant and watery, she smiles, rests her hand on the pouch.

"Be careful," I say. "Gentle touches only."

She nods and moves her hand to my shoulder to keep her balance, and I want to weep because when we get home I will move out. Because when I move out I will see her only every other weekend. Because I worry that what I am doing is wrong, and I do it anyway. I pull a too-big sweatshirt over Claudia's head, the purple one I bought that morning in the gift shop, with large rainbow letters spelling out *Kauai*. All week she has been asking for it.

Outside the hotel, the cab is waiting for us, and as the driver weaves in and out of traffic, Claudia names all the colors of the sunrise.

When we arrive, I pay the cab driver and he removes the luggage from the trunk.

"Can you walk?" I ask Claudia. "Like a big girl? Just through security?"

This, too, is something I don't like to remember and can't manage to forget. The way I used that line— *like a big girl*—because I know she can't refuse this particular challenge. I know she will do it, walk right through the threshold, mention nothing of the pouch that is strapped to her body. And she does, and no one stops her because if you could see her, if you could see how sweet and tired and sick she looks, you too would let her through.

At our gate I bring Claudia to the chairs closest to the window, where she likes to count the airplanes. But today she doesn't count. She curls up in the seat next to me, puts her head in my lap.

"How are you feeling?" I ask her.

"I think it's working," she whispers, touching her chest.

I cover her body with my flannel shirt, and I tell her to open her mouth. I place the thermometer under her tongue and push her hair away from her face. The couple next to me—sunburned, smelling of coconut—hold hands and watch us. They are both wearing shorts and sandals, and I know they will be cold when they arrive wherever it is they are going. I nod at them but don't engage, and when it is time, I pull the thermometer from Claudia's mouth. Her temperature has risen one degree since we left the hotel.

101.7.

―――

I can pretend sometimes, when I reach this part of the memory, that the pouch is empty. That I've just told her a small fib, have given her something to focus on that isn't her headache or her temperature or her sore throat or her legs, which feel a little bit like they are on fire, she says.

But it's not true, and what those tanned and sandaled tourists think of me in that moment isn't entirely right, either, because I'm not the caring, attentive father they think they see. Inside that velvet pouch, strapped to my daughter's chest, I've placed the two falcon eggs. Each one—if I can keep them alive—will sell for as much as five thousand dollars. And each sale, I reason, will allow me to travel with Claudia, will allow me to be alone with her, to make memories, to be a good father to her even though I no longer want to be a good husband to her mother. I am imagining a trip to Florida, to bring her to Disney World. A flight to Europe, maybe. Or even somewhere in Mexico. It hardly matters. With the money from these eggs, I will take her wherever she wants to go. We will do whatever it is she wants to do. Just to be together. When I discovered these eggs—at the end of our trip, at the end of a sleep-deprived week—my reasoning seemed sound.

If this were the worst of it, if this were all I did that day—used my daughter's fevered body to warm those eggs—then maybe I could, all these years later, finally forgive myself.

On the plane, it is the older of the two flight attendants who notices Claudia is ill, and she brings me a cup with two chewable tablets inside.

"I'm not really supposed to do this," she whispers. "But I always have them in my purse. For my own daughter." She brings Claudia another blanket, a container of apple juice, and a special gift—a pin, just like the one the captain wears. Airplane wings. I secure the wings to her sweatshirt. I push her hair out of her face. I slip the two aspirin into my pocket.

———

What you are probably thinking: no way. No way a father would do this. No way a father would withhold that medicine.

Do you think I haven't had this thought? Do you think, in the days when I can't forget what I've done, in the nights when I lie awake in bed replaying this moment again and again, that I haven't wished for this to be true, for you to be right?

This trip—it's the first and only time I have ever transported living eggs on my own. All those eggs at home, those one thousand eggs sitting side by side, clutch by clutch, labeled and dated, stored in the maple cabinet? They all came from my grandfather when he died, which isn't to say I didn't want them. I did. I have many memories of hunting for those eggs when I was a boy, searching for nests with him on the weekends: pipits, common thrushes, painted buntings, red-winged blackbirds, brown-headed cowbirds. On and on. Sometimes we climbed steep mountains to find them. Sometimes he'd give me a flashlight and send me into caves alone, my body still nimble and small enough to thread through narrow openings. Sometimes I was scared, but I'd lift those eggs out of the nests, hand them off to my grandfather, and at home I'd watch as he poked a hole in each one, inserted a straw, blew them hollow, and placed them on the windowsill to dry. He always let me put them in the maple cabinet. He always let me write the date.

As we worked, my grandfather used to tell me stories about men who flew to Wales and climbed the cliffs near Aberdare, loaded down with carabiners, ropes, incubators, and insulated bags, in search of the rarest eggs they could find. He used to tell me about the man in England who fell to his death trying to reach a clutch of golden eagles on the side of a cliff, without any ropes to help him down. I imagine he told me these stories as a warning, as a way to distinguish what he was doing from what they were doing. My grandfather did it, he said, in the name of preservation, in the name of science. He believed one day these birds would all disappear, that they would be hunted to extinction or poisoned by crop sprays or driven away by out-of-control development. I didn't pretend to understand what he meant in those long, meandering speeches about providing artifacts for future generations, and I only understand the irony of it now. My grandfather's obsession with these birds and their eggs, his strange impulse to kill the very thing he most loved, to lock it away in a large maple cabinet so he might keep it forever.

———

I am asleep on the final leg of our flight, somewhere between Los Angeles and Boston, when the seat starts to shake and I grab my armrest because I think it is turbulence. It takes me a moment to realize it is Claudia. Her body is seizing. In a panic, I try to wake her. I put her face in my hands, my lips to her forehead. "Oh god," I say. Oh god, oh god, oh god.

I jam the thermometer into her mouth once more. 104.1.

I drop the two aspirin on her pink, pink tongue. I beg her to chew. When she doesn't, I move her jaw for her. The woman next to me puts her hand on my shoulder, asks if there is anything she can do.

"Please," I say, not to the woman but to Claudia. And then I stick my finger into Claudia's mouth, fish out the pills, and put them under her tongue. I check every few seconds until they dissolve.

When the plane lands in Boston an ambulance is waiting for us. Already I have removed the pouch from her body, have tucked it under my own shirt. I have removed Claudia's socks and her sweatshirt and even her pants because a nurse three rows in front of us said it was important to cool her body, let it breathe. Someone brought bags of ice. Someone put them under Claudia's arms, at the back of her neck, on her groin. I remember almost nothing of that last hour in the air, but I remember that feeling of the pouch on my skin, my body nowhere near warm enough to keep the eggs alive for long.

---

Claudia's mother is waiting for us when we arrive at the hospital. It takes two days for Claudia's fever to come down.

On the second day, standing next to my daughter's hospital bed, the doctor asks us to step out of the room. We follow her into the hall, and she looks down at the files in her hands and then back up at us.

"It's rare," she says, "but the fever has caused permanent damage in her right ear. She hasn't lost all ability to hear, but she has lost much of it. We estimate about eighty-five percent."

There are questions. Lots of them. But I don't even know who is asking or who is answering. I hear my own voice. My ex-wife's. The doctor's. I stand in the hallway of the hospital and all I can think is that it is too bright. These fluorescent lights are much too bright. The doctor leaves us, and we stand there for what feels like a long time, and then we are beside Claudia's bed, where she is asleep under crisp white sheets.

What I tell my ex-wife next: "I'm giving you full custody. I'm signing over my rights, all of them. Claudia is better off without me in her life."

"Don't be so dramatic," she says.

But when I insist she softens and asks if I am certain. I am.

———

In the painful, lonely years that follow, even though I am not legally obligated to do so, I send Claudia a check on the first of every month. Only once does my ex-wife ask me to stop, saying it muddies the terms of our agreement. I have no rights to Claudia and no obligation to her either.

I ignore her request and she continues to cash the checks. I pretend it helps, this monthly ritual of writing the check, sealing the envelope, affixing the stamp. And I know how it looks. God, I know it looks like I am trying to buy her off, pay back some impossible debt. But it has little to do with the money. I'm only looking for a different ending to this story, a different conclusion to the memory, because no one can live with the memory of their daughter in a hospital bed, her body hooked up to tubes, the beeping of the machines.

I was so young. Just twenty-nine. I cling to this. I was so, so young. Sometimes I catch myself saying it aloud, to no one.

I don't mean I was too young to know better about the eggs, her fever. There is no excuse for that. I mean I was too young when I signed those papers. Too young to know what it means to give up custody, to turn from your daughter like that.

I still have my grandfather's eggs. They are in the base-
ment now, still stored in the maple cabinet.

Rarely do I go down there to look at them anymore.
Recently, I called the Museum of Natural History, hoping to make good on my grandfather's desire to donate
the eggs. The man I spoke with counseled me to stay
quiet about them.

"It is illegal," he explained, "to steal eggs out of nests.
It probably wasn't when your grandfather collected them,
but things have changed. The best thing to do, the cleanest way to proceed, is to write it in as a donation to us in
your will."

"I'm only fifty-two," I explained. "I'd like them out of
my house now."

"If it comes to us from your will, it would be a clean
donation. Otherwise, there would be legal consequences."

"Like a fine?" I asked.

I am willing to pay a fine.

"No," he said. "Like jail."

I want to hedge and tell him I had nothing to do
with the eggs, that it was my grandfather alone who was
responsible for this collection, that I couldn't possibly be
expected to pay the consequences of his actions. I want to
tell him that, but I can't.

It was Claudia who asked about the magic pouch
when we left the hospital. She wanted to know what was
in it. She wanted to know how I had saved her. I opened
the bottom drawer and showed her the two eggs. My
attempt to keep them alive had failed. She hadn't been
warm enough, or I hadn't been warm enough, and so

after I returned home, while we were waiting for her to recover, I held them over the sink, blew out the centers, and added them to the cabinet. When I showed Claudia, she said they were the only eggs without a date. She asked if she could write it, and I handed her a pen.

———

When Claudia turns eighteen she can contact me if she wants to. That's what the papers say, which means every day after July 18, 2011, I am met with a new kind of punishment, a different end to an already painful conclusion, a silence I can't fill.

———

All the ways I have imagined our reunion: we might bump into each other at the grocery store, at the park, on the sidewalk, at the little beach by the bay, out on the Cape, at the aquarium, at my favorite restaurant, at her favorite restaurant, at the library or a bookstore, in line at the post office or the DMV as we are both renewing an expired license.

I have imagined the particulars of each of these scenarios, but when I see her name in my work email, eleven years after she turns eighteen, long after I have given up on the fantasy of our reunion, I freeze because I haven't imagined this particular situation and I'm not sure it is real and the blank subject line has me worried and I let the cursor hang for a moment over her name.

Claudia Brooks.

It is not my last name. It is her mother's last name and I wonder immediately when this happened. How soon after I signed the papers did her mother make the change? Or did Claudia do it, years later? And why?

I click open the email. She is in town for a conference. She has some time between meetings. There's a café in the hotel where she is staying. If I'm available.

———

I am the first to arrive. I order a coffee and two chocolate chip cookies. I sip my drink and wait, although I don't have to wait long because I see Claudia coming through the lobby, and the first thing I notice is that her hair is more brown than blond now, and that although her hair is long in every picture I've been able to find on the internet, it is now a short bob, just like her mother's was when we were married. I adjust the tie at my throat. I pull my sport coat tight to hide my stomach. I push my coffee cup to the edge of the table, straighten the plate of cookies. I stand up and wave at my daughter.

It is only when Claudia sees me and approaches the table that I realize the man behind her, the one in the striped suit, is with her.

On the way to the hotel, I decided I would offer my daughter a hug rather than a handshake, but with this man present, I lose my nerve and stick out my hand as Claudia approaches. She takes it, and I am surprised that her grasp is limp.

"This is Lucian," she says.

I expect her to say more, but she doesn't. I take the hand he extends and then he pulls a chair from a nearby table, adds it to our two-top.

"Thank you for reaching out," I say to Claudia.

She looks at me but says nothing. She smiles a little. She shifts in her seat, puts her purse on the floor, and picks it up again and places it in her lap.

"It's really nice to see you," I say.

I had prepared myself for silence, a lull in the conversation. I'd made a mental list of questions to ask Claudia, thinking up ways to draw her out, ways to make her feel comfortable. I had even prepared myself for the possibility of outright hostility. But I hadn't expected this. This stranger, this man who orders two coffees—one for himself, one for Claudia—when the waitress arrives. He doesn't ask Claudia what she wants before he orders.

When the waitress leaves, it is just the three of us sitting at the too-small table, our knees nearly touching. I look over at Lucian and wonder what he has heard of me. I wonder what he thinks of a man who abandons his young daughter.

"You've heard about my mom, I assume?" Claudia says.

I nod. "How's she feeling?"

Claudia shakes her head. "She's not in pain at least. They've got her on a lot of medication."

"Can I do anything?" I say.

Claudia leans over the table. "Sorry?" she says. She has turned the left side of her face to me, and cupped her hand to her ear.

It's then that I notice all the noise around us. The woman to my right, who is dragging her spoon along the bottom of her soup bowl. On the other side of us, a man in a black suit shouts into his computer about high international shipping rates. The music coming from the speakers above us is much too loud for this small café. Across the room, someone steams milk, slams the espresso arm against the trash can, calls for her coworker to bring more beans.

I also lean in across the table, aware of how close our bodies are.

"Is there anything I can do?" I say, this time more loudly.

My daughter leans back in her chair and looks away from me. She glances at Lucian, lifting the coffee cup to her mouth, and when she does this I can see her bottom lip is trembling. I understand clearly in this moment why my daughter is reaching out to me now. Because her mother is about to die. Because we are family. And this gives me hope.

"It's been hard," she says, placing her coffee on the table. "But we're managing. We always have."

I want to reach out to hug her, to take her hand, to ease the pain of what's to come, to apologize. When she reaches her own hand out, though, it's not for me but for the cookie sitting between us. I smile at her.

"It was a guess, of course, that it would still be a favorite."

She nods, pushing the plate closer to Lucian, and I watch carefully to see if their hands touch or if he smiles at her or if she smiles back. I wonder who they are to each other, whether they are simply coworkers or whether there is something more here, a friendship closing in on love, a love closing in on marriage. They give away nothing.

Claudia reaches into her purse, takes out a tissue, and blows her nose. And then Lucian's hand is on her back, and I have no right to my feelings of protection, no right to tell her to be careful with this one, that there's something untrustworthy about him, that I sensed it as soon as he sat down.

When Claudia pulls her tissue away from her nose and smiles, she asks: "Do you still have the eggs?"

She is, I sense, trying to get us on safer ground. Away from her dying mother. Away from my departure. I nod, say nothing more, and she wipes at her nose again with the tissue, shoves it back into her purse, and turns to Lucian. "It was this giant cabinet," she tells him, her arms out wide. "Full of bird eggs. Thousands of them. I loved looking at them."

Lucian is smiling at her, and I think for sure they must be dating.

"We used to go out hunting for them," she says. "Sometimes in the middle of the night we'd hike to the top of a mountain and wear our headlamps and slip into little caves to collect them."

I don't stop Claudia to correct her, to tell her she has it wrong—so, so wrong—because she is animated now, despite the fact that her eyes are still wet. Lucian looks at me, drawing conclusions that aren't true.

"And once," she says, keeping her attention on Lucian, "he harnessed me up and lowered me down near the edge of a cliff to get some egg. There was a black cape, wasn't there? Or was it red?" She turns to me but doesn't give me time to answer. "You tied it around my neck, I think, and told me I could fly, that only I could rescue those eggs so they wouldn't be blown away by the incoming storm. I believed it. I really did."

It goes on like this a little longer. Claudia telling stories that aren't true but with the conviction that they are. Lucian attentive, listening, smiling. He asks all the right questions at each pause, filling every silence before I can interject.

"You must have been so scared," he says, laughing at the image of Claudia out there on the ledge in a cape, thinking she could fly.

"Terrified!" she says, but she is laughing, her smile wide, her teeth perfectly straight, and I realize she must have had braces.

"It wasn't entirely like that," I say, finding my way in now, leaning across the table to make sure Claudia can hear me. They turn to me, each waiting for me to go on, but as soon as I begin, I see Claudia cup her hand behind her ear, palm pink from gripping the coffee cup, fingers small and delicate just as I remember them, impossibly thin for a grown woman. I stop myself from explaining. The one thing I manage to add: "I haven't collected eggs in decades."

I sit back, pulling my coffee cup to my mouth even though it is empty. An uncomfortable silence follows. Lucian looks at his watch. He pushes his chair back.

"I'm sorry," he says. "My panel. It starts in twenty minutes."

As he stands, I am relieved because I want to talk to Claudia alone—about her mother and about the work she is doing here, which she hasn't even mentioned—but then she is standing too, and they are each pulling out their wallets, dropping money on the table. I want this to mean they are not together.

"No," I say, pushing their money back at them. "I insist. Please let me pay."

---

I drive home along the Charles River, to Heidi, my wife of nineteen years, and to my kids—Gwen, sixteen, and Isaiah, who has just turned thirteen. Tonight we are celebrating his birthday.

It is a bright autumn afternoon, and as I drive west along the river, the sun is already hanging low near the horizon. The drivers around me find their sunglasses, pull down their visors, hold up hands to shield their eyes from the light, and we all creep forward in rush hour traffic. Runners pass my car. Mothers with strollers pass me. Bikers and a few people on Rollerblades, and even one on roller skates. They all pass me. Behind them, on the river, a team of rowers in matching jackets heave themselves down the glittering water, their arms and legs moving in perfect union. For a moment, as my car inches forward, it seems as though everything has fallen away. The cars, the leafless trees, the vendors along the water, the runners—it has all dissolved, and it seems as though the boat is dragging me along.

Behind me, someone turns up a radio. The bass pounds me back into the moment. The day returns to what it is. I find myself near tears.

How many details Claudia has gotten wrong. It's true we sometimes drove up to the Rockport cliffs to watch the seabirds. But the harness? The cape? That was a story I used to tell her each night before bed because she loved to hear it, how my grandfather used to take me out in the dark of the night, harness me up and lower me down. And that fear? That fear was mine, too.

But I will let her have this story. I will let them believe this is the worst I have done. How grateful I am for this small mercy, her faulty memory.

# DIDI

WHEN MY BROTHER calls it's about his daughter, Didi. She is seventeen, out of control. Total nightmare to be around. Lacks respect for the rules. Out all night with friends he doesn't know, with boys she's just met.

"She came home at three thirty this morning in a pair of high heels," he says. "Last week she returned without any shoes at all."

It's not just her footwear. Don't even get him started about her shorts. Her shirts, too. Too short, too tight, big bold words printed across the front: *Juicy* and *Unwrap Me* and the one that stunned him into silence, drove him to pick up the phone and call me: *Save Water, Shower with Someone's Boyfriend.*

I laugh. It's not funny, he tells me. Nothing about this is funny.

He's tried everything. He's bought her new clothes. T-shirts—thick T-shirts, cotton T-shirts—and by the next day she's taken liberties with the scissors. Gashes across the back. A deep *V* into the neck. The arms are gone, the front tied in a knot above her belly button. Which is pierced. Did he mention that? That his daughter lay flat on her back to let some guy drive a hole through her stomach with a needle he sterilized on his stove?

163

"Her mother," he says. Her poor mother. She doesn't even know what to do anymore. At wit's end. Haunted by images of Didi facedown in a ditch, shirt up over her head, her body bloody and cold.

What my brother doesn't say and what we both know: he doesn't deserve a child like this, but I probably do. Maybe I feel bad for her. Maybe I sense in this phone call that he wants to send her away to a place far off in the wilderness, far away from everything, to dig ditches in the desert or climb mountains with other troubled teens. All in the name of tough love.

"Okay," I say, "fine. Send her here. Just for a month. Just to reset."

Immediately, I regret it, realizing my brother is probably taking advantage of me.

My husband tells me I'm being paranoid, a little selfish.

"It's just a month," he says. "We can do anything for a month."

———

When Didi arrives, I take a week off from work, leave my lab in the hands of my graduate students, give them a single instruction: don't let anything die. The first thing I notice is that Didi is small, makes herself even smaller by curling up on a single couch cushion. She crosses her arms even when standing in large rooms. Tucks her legs under her body when she sits at the kitchen table, pushes her silverware under the lip of her dinner plate to take up even less space. Everything about her is scrunched, compact. And there is no sign of those clothes. What Didi wears is boring at best, nothing worth commenting on or worrying about. Ill-fitting blue jeans. Baggy tank tops. Sometimes she wears a baseball hat that comes down over her ears and makes her look even younger than she is.

Still, no matter what she wears, Didi's days are no longer her own. I take her with me to run errands. I tour her around Westport. We see movies in the middle of the day. I drive her out to the beach so she can see the Pacific coast. Just once, because I can't help it, I take her to the lab with me so I can check on the shipment of mantis shrimp that has just arrived. I show her one of the buckets, a single shrimp inside it. People are normally surprised by how big they are, but Didi doesn't move away, doesn't wince, so I pick one up.

"This thing has the fastest animal movement on the planet," I tell her. "They use this appendage like a crossbow. Wind it up real tight and then let it go, killing prey in a single whack."

"You do tests on them?" she asks. "Like experiments and things?"

I nod. "We've clocked that movement at eighty-three miles an hour."

"Does it hurt them? When you test?"

I return the shrimp to the bucket. I don't tell her about our next study, the one our lab is already behind on, where we will remove their eyes from their bodies to better understand how they see color.

"Well," I say. "We're getting better at controlling for that."

At home, Didi reads. Occasionally she'll get up to get a glass of water, to fetch something to eat, to find a sunnier spot in the house. She tears through the books she's brought. Biographies of musicians. Short histories of Western philosophy. When she finally puts the books down to come to the table and eat, she asks lofty questions. How can we all be more like Simone Weil? Like Mother Teresa? I bite my lip. When she finishes philosophizing, Didi offers impulsive confessions. She's never swum in a lake before. She's never been on a roller coaster that goes backward. She taught herself to ride a bike.

At the end of the first week, I tell Evan I think it is going to be okay. "She's a little weird," I say, "but it might actually be fun to have her around." I climb into bed beside him. I run my hand across his chest and hold on to his shoulder. Even though he's showered, he still smells like the nursery—the trees he repots, the garden herbs he sells to customers.

"I don't know," Evan says. "Something about her makes me nervous."

"What do you mean?"

"Have you noticed—" he says. He stops. We listen as a door down the hall opens and closes. Didi is in the bathroom. He lowers his voice to a whisper. "It's like she's set up mirrors all around her. Like she's constantly watching herself every time she moves."

The next morning I call my brother. I ask him if he is sure he sent the right child.

"Don't let your guard down," he says. "This is what she does."

———

In Didi's second week, I return to the lab because two of our specimens have already died and my graduate students can't figure out why. Before I leave, I write my office number on a piece of paper. Under it, my cell phone number and the number to the department just in case she can't reach me and needs to leave a message with the lab assistant. I magnet it to the refrigerator and tell her it is there. She says she'll call if she needs anything.

"Or just let Evan know," I tell her. "He took the day off, so he'll be around."

When I return that afternoon, I find her in the living room, curled up on a single cushion of the couch. She barely looks up from the book in her lap when I walk in. Finally, when I interrupt her, she turns to face me, blinks her eyes.

"Fine," she says, as though this word speaks to an entire day.

When I pry, she sighs, puts her finger between the pages to save her place, and shows me the cover. Another biography. A ballet dancer I've never heard of.

"Do you still dance?" I ask her, remembering all the recitals I missed.

"No," she says. "I quit when I was ten."

"You used to love it," I say.

She shrugs. "I was bored. And everyone else got better."

She puts the book on the couch and gets up to go to the fridge.

"Should we go to the pool?" I ask. I'm doubting even her belly button ring now. I think maybe my brother has made that up as well. "Free swim starts at seven."

Didi returns from the kitchen. She has an apple in her hand.

"I didn't bring a bathing suit," she says.

"I have lots. You can borrow one."

Didi scans me from head to toe, takes a bite of her apple.

"Or we could run down to the mall," I say, "and get you a new one if you want."

"I'm good," she says. She picks up the book and keeps reading.

"Where'd that come from?" I ask. "I don't remember buying apples."

"Grocery store," she says. "I walked down there today."

"Alone?" I ask.

"Yeah."

"The whole way?"

"It's not that far."

———

"I must have been on the phone with my parents," Evan says that night as he clears the table. "I didn't even know she was gone."

"You can't do that," I whisper. "When you're here, you have to watch her." My hands are deep in soapy water, and I am scrubbing the forks with a sponge.

"Val, she's seventeen," he says, slipping our dirty plates into the sink.

"You said you were okay with this. You said you were fine using your sick days, keeping an eye on her."

"And I did. We had lunch together. I checked on her twice. I made some calls. She read."

He dips a washcloth in the water, wipes the counter, and moves to the table.

"But we agreed you'd call me if she needed something. And you even said that you were a little worried. That whole mirror thing. You were concerned."

"We didn't need anything. I talked to my parents. Called my sister. Anyway, it was the middle of the day. How much trouble can she actually get in?"

I turn to him, hands soapy.

"That's not the point," I say.

"Then what is the point?"

"That something *could* have happened to her. That she *could* have gotten into trouble."

"Like what?" he says. "It's Westport. It's not like we live in the most thrilling place."

He hangs the wet washcloth on the hook above the sink. I grab his hand, but he doesn't look at me.

"What does that have to do with it?" I say.

"It's nothing. I'm just saying there isn't much trouble for her to get into here. It's quiet."

"You mean boring. You mean it's not Chicago."

Finally, he turns to me.

"Listen, can we just drop this? Please? She's fine. We're fine. Maybe tomorrow we can set up a camera and you can observe us both from work, turn us into one of your little experiments, make sure we're doing everything exactly the way you want us to."

"Don't mock me," I say.

—

The mirror thing. I want Evan to explain it further. I want him to point it out to me so I can see what he sees because all I see is a girl pulling her knees to her chin, her arms around her shins. Like she's trying to tuck in her heart. She takes up less and less space at the table each morning. Sits on her hands as we watch movies in the living room. When she takes popcorn from the bowl she chooses one kernel at a time. She lets it dissolve in her mouth before she chews. When I go into her bedroom each morning, it looks like she hasn't shifted in bed, like she didn't move from the first place her body touched. This morning, when I look in on her, I see she is sleeping on top of the quilt with no covers at all.

When she comes out, I am at the table eating breakfast and I ask her if the bed is okay, if she is comfortable in the guest room. She says yes, it's great. She hasn't slept so well in a long time.

"Do you not sleep well at home?" I ask.

"Not really," she says. "Mom refuses to run the AC."

"Are you too warm here?" I ask. "We can put the AC on at night."

"That's okay. I'm mostly comfortable," she says. "Although I might open my window a little tonight, if you don't mind."

---

When I get home from the lab they are both on the couch watching the TV on mute. I am late; at the end of the day, I successfully removed a specimen's hard, bead-like eye, but when I tried to transfer it to a test tube, rushing, it popped out and I lost it. On the TV, I see footage of an attack somewhere in Iran, and Didi is telling Evan about the Iranian poet she has been reading. He looks genuinely interested. I don't interrupt.

Instead, I put my bag down quietly, taking a seat on the chair beside Evan, and listen as she talks about the way the poet broke a traditional form to make a political statement about the injustice of the current regime. When Didi finishes, she goes to her bedroom to get her coat, and Evan raises his eyebrows and mouths *wow*. He leans over to kiss me on my forehead, my nose, my lips, and when Didi returns we all walk into town for pizza.

The waiter is excited to see us. He scolds Evan and me for not coming more often, and he welcomes Didi to town, to the restaurant. He tells her everything on the menu is good, that she can't go wrong, which is exactly the same thing he tells us every time we come here. Whatever we order, it is always, in his words, a very fine choice.

Didi defers to us. She will eat anything, she says, and so we order two pizzas and a salad to share. As we wait, I try not to watch the TV behind Didi and Evan where they are showing the aftermath of the bombing. It's bad. More than four hundred dead. They keep showing the same image of a young boy with a bloody face. I'm certain it's not his blood. His face isn't at all scratched, but the boy is clearly stunned. I try to refocus on Evan and Didi's conversation. He is wondering about future plans. Has she thought about college?

"Not a lot," she says. "I'm thinking about taking a gap year."

"Be careful," Evan says. "Those don't always work out."

He is speaking from experience. She asks him what he means.

"I had plans," he says. "I was going to backpack around Europe with my girlfriend. Take the train from Spain to Italy to Germany. Up through Scandinavia. Had it all planned out. Had the plane ticket in my pocket. Two weeks out and she dumps me. Turns out she had applied to college and was going to Boston without me. She was waiting to tell me until all her financial aid came through. That trip abroad? That was her backup plan. *I* was her backup plan."

"So you didn't go?" Didi asks. "Why didn't you just go alone?"

"Wasn't like that. Wasn't about the trip. It was about her. Us."

"And the girlfriend?"

Evan looks at me with a grin.

"She came running back, eventually."

"No!" Didi says. "It was you! You did that to him, Aunt Val?! That's so cruel!"

Evan smiles even wider and turns back to Didi.

"I was okay," he says. "She did the smart thing."

The waiter delivers both pizzas and the salad to the table. He serves us each our first piece. We toast with our water glasses.

"To gap years," I say, and they both laugh.

"Well," Evan says, "you've heard my warning. But what do you have planned? Hopefully nothing with a cruel-hearted high school sweetheart."

Didi shakes her head.

"No," she says. "Nothing like that. I don't even know really. I just thought it might be nice to have a break from school for a little bit."

She picks the mushrooms off her pizza. Puts them in a tidy pile on the side of her plate.

"It's kind of nice here," she says, not looking up at us. She moves on to the sausage, puts it in a separate pile. "It's quiet, at least. Not as hot as Texas."

She cuts her crust into bird-sized bites and chews one slowly.

Calculated, I think. Maybe that's what Evan means with the whole mirror thing. Every move. Every word. Every gesture. It is all very calculated.

"Yeah, Westport is nice," Evan says.

The waiter returns. He asks Didi if everything is okay. If there was something wrong with the pizza. If he can get her anything else.

"It was so good," she says, handing him the plate, her pizza picked over but not eaten. "So delicious."

---

At the end of the meal, I suggest we walk home and have dessert on the porch. It is a beautiful night. A coastal breeze has come inland. We pay up. As we leave, the waiter runs after us with the box of pizza we left on the table. He apologizes to Didi again, is concerned she hasn't had enough to eat.

"I'm worried you will float away," he says.

She promises him she had plenty to eat. She pats her stomach to convince him.

As we walk home, Didi and Evan are back on the Iranian poet. More lofty questions: What do you think is the role of the poet during such violence? What is the role of *any* artist, for that matter?

At home, Evan brings a bottle of wine onto the porch. Didi says she needs to call her parents.

"It's only eight," I say. "Come eat pie with us."

"I promised I'd check in."

"One piece. Look," I say, holding up the plate. "From the bakery. Look how beautiful it is."

She agrees, reluctantly. On the porch, she sits on the edge of her seat, picking at the cherries while Evan and I each take a second piece, a second glass of wine. She finishes it though, the entire slice of pie. And then she clears our dishes for us. I hear her at the sink washing them. She comes back out to say she's turning in. She's going to go to her room, call her dad. She will probably read after that.

I smile at her. "Tell him we say hi."

Evan and I talk about our days—the shipment of hostas that arrived at the garden center, how he had to unload them alone; how I lost the shrimp eye and am behind on our data collection—and I hear Didi's voice coming through the night. It's soft, but I can tell it's the voice of someone who is happy. It's also a young voice. So young. Almost babyish, as though she is talking to a dog, coaxing it to her with a treat. Her window is open. I stop talking. I am straining to hear her words.

"Hello?" Evan says, waving in my direction. "Where are you, Val?"

"Have you ever heard a girl talk to her parents like that? In a voice like that?"

"You would be a terrible mother," he says.

"Wouldn't I? Overbearing. Overprotective."

"A total spy," he says.

This has been a joke between us. I don't believe it is untrue.

"Still," I say. "Admit it. It's a little weird. The whole thing at dinner. Picking at her food like that."

He admits it. Yes, it was strange. We stay up late, long after Didi's voice goes quiet and her light shuts off.

"You had to tell her that story," I say. I am smiling.

"We could still do it," he says. "Take a gap year. Travel around by train. Find ourselves and all that."

This isn't the first time he has proposed the idea. He brought it with him when he eventually followed me to Boston. And to Minneapolis for grad school. And to Chicago for my postdoc. And now here to Westport for my job. For him to bring it up now, I know it means he is bored, restless, generally unsatisfied with the fact that we have landed in a town he doesn't like but is, once again, making work.

"Maybe for my sabbatical," I say.

"In five years?" he asks, exasperated.

I know it is the wrong thing to say. His has been the harder path, I know this. The constant moving. The random jobs he's accepted not because they will lead anywhere but because they pay rent. The year working construction in Boston. The year as a substitute teacher. Three years waiting tables. And now the garden center, where he works alongside high school students, unloading trees and plants, hauling them into place at the nursery and then hauling them into the cars and trucks of customers.

"What if I *had* gone?" Evan asks. It is his attempt at a lofty question. "What if I had boarded that plane and spent the year traveling alone? What if I hadn't been there when you came home that first Christmas?"

I have no answer. I sip my wine.

———

I look in on Didi after midnight, just before I go to bed, and she is there, her back to the wall, curled up in a ball, the window open, the breeze cool, covers pushed to the bottom of the bed.

I remember a neighbor in Chicago. A woman with triplets, all boys, eighteen months old. We had just moved in, and I was unpacking boxes one day when she came running to our door. She was locked out. She had slipped out to have a cigarette—*Not even a full one*, she said. *Just two drags*—and the door clicked behind her. Her boys were inside. She had already called the landlord. He was on the way with a key. We stood at her living room window and watched her triplets slink around on their stomachs, rise to their hands and knees, and begin to crawl. There was no gate to the kitchen. The bathroom door was wide-open. A set of wooden stairs led to the second floor. She was crying, cursing herself for being so stupid, for being so care-less, tapping on the window, trying to get the boys to look at her. I grabbed a rock from the yard. *If they get too close to the kitchen or the stairs*, I told her, *I'll put it through the window*. She nodded. She sang to the boys through the glass. They crawled toward us. They smiled at their mother. They extended their arms, wanting to be picked up. They cried. Finally, the landlord arrived with the key, and I walked back to my house with a racing heart, the heavy rock still in my hand, thinking this must be what parenthood is like all the time.

---

In the morning, before I leave for work, I knock gently. It's supposed to reach ninety degrees today, and my plan is to go to the lab for a few hours, come home at lunch, and bring Didi to the store so she can get a bathing suit and we can spend the afternoon at the lake. That's what my calendar says will happen.

I knock again, but Didi doesn't respond, and so I knock a little louder, and then I let myself in. She isn't there. I'm thinking that she must have slipped into the bathroom after me. She woke early because she went to sleep early. I move down the hall to the bathroom, but she isn't there either. I check the back porch, which is as we left it last night. Two wineglasses. An empty bottle of red.

Even when I say it to Evan it doesn't really seem possible.

Her clothes. Her makeup. Gone. Her shampoo is gone from the shower. Her retainer from the bathroom sink. Hair ties. Everything, gone.

There's nothing in the closet, no shoes by the door, and all I can say—all I can *think* to say—is, "She was just here, she was just here. She can't just disappear."

Evan already has the phone in his hand. He is calling Didi, and I can hear the phone ring. It goes to voice mail, a mechanical female voice rattling off the digits of Didi's number. Evan hangs up.

"Try again," I tell him.

"Val," he says.

"Do it," I tell him.

He is scrolling through names in his contact list. He presses my brother's name.

"No," I say, taking the phone from him. "Not yet."

"Maybe he's heard from her. Maybe she said something last night when she talked to him."

"She didn't call him last night," I say. "No girl talks to her father with a voice like that. You heard her. You heard that voice."

He nods. He knows I'm right.

We sit on the couch and think of all the possibilities, and then Evan leaves the house to check the bus stop, every business in town.

Before he closes the door, almost as an afterthought, he instructs me to do what I already know I must: "Call your brother."

Of course he hasn't heard from her.

While he yells at me, I walk out onto the driveway and stand there as though she'll show up while I'm on the phone, so I can tell him it's all been a big mistake, a huge misunderstanding. I consider all the things my brother has told me about her, all the things he's telling me again.

Teenagers do this stuff every day, I hear myself telling him. Teenagers disappear and come back when they're hungry.

She's not a dog, he is saying. She's not a *goddamn dog*.

"I just mean—"

"I thought things were going well. I thought everyone was having a *great* time."

"They were," I say. "We are."

It goes on like this until Evan returns, without Didi, and he gets out of the car and tells me there's no sign of her anywhere, that it might be time to call the police.

———

Two officers arrive within minutes. I have seen one of them—the woman—in uniform, walking up and down streets, putting tickets on people's windshields. How I hated her in those moments when she just stood watching the meter, counting down, waiting for the time to run out, so she could print a ticket and slide it under the wiper. Now, it's not hate I feel but an intense need to speak directly to her rather than the other officer—a man I've never seen before.

"My niece is gone," I say as she leads me back inside, taking out her notepad and her pen, asking me to tell them when we last saw her, who in the area she knows, how long she has been here, what she was last wearing.

"What does that matter?" I reply. "What she was wearing?"

The woman looks at me. She doesn't skip a beat.

"For identification purposes," she says. Before I can apologize, Evan is trying to describe her clothes. Baggy jeans. Loose T-shirts. Sometimes a ball cap. As he speaks, all I can think is, *Please let her be okay. Please, please. Let this nice woman, Officer Peterson, find her.*

The police ask to look around. They are in and out of our bedroom. In and out of Didi's room. The bathroom. The porch. They ask about the bottle of wine. The glasses. They check windows and doors. I follow them around the house. I follow this woman, especially. She inquires about locks and alarm systems.

"Do you always keep it open?" she says of Didi's window.

It takes me a second to make sense of her question.

"You think someone came in and took her?" I ask.

"We have to consider everything," she says. "But between you and me, I doubt it."

I want this woman to tell me again and again in her matter-of-fact voice, just as she's telling me now: "Listen, this happens a lot. Teenagers leave. Disappear for a day or two. They usually show up."

And that's what I was trying to say to my brother. Not that they return when they're hungry but that they usually show up.

"Her father thinks she's a bad kid, but he's wrong," I say. "She tries to make herself small. She moves from one sunny spot to another all day, reading biographies of ballerinas and books about Iranian poets. And when she moves, it's like she's set up mirrors all around her. Like she's always watching herself."

Officer Peterson looks up from her pad. "What do you mean?" she says.

I don't tell her that I think Didi's actions seem calculated, borderline manipulative. I don't want her to think badly of my niece. *I* don't want to think badly of her.

"I only mean that she's careful," I say. "Incredibly alert."

I catch her looking behind me, beyond me, and I turn and see Evan showing the other officer where we store the bikes. The shed is full, both bikes parked in their separate corners.

I pick up the phone because it is ringing, and I am certain it will be Didi. But it's my brother, and he is listing off times, and I am confused until I realize he is on a computer, looking at flights, booking something to Portland.

My brother has never been on a plane. He rarely leaves east Texas. He works on the oil rig where our father worked, where our grandfather worked. He has taken care of our sick parents. Has given everything he has to his daughter. Has worked long hours to give her private dance lessons.

"Listen, you might be overreacting," I tell him, trying to project calm, trying to remain confident. "She'll probably show up."

He hangs up on me.

The police leave. I go into Didi's room. I pull back the covers on the bed. I look for anything she might have left behind, any kind of clue. Suddenly I am furious at my brother. He knew. He knew she would do this, and he sent her here anyway. Surely he is also a little responsible for this. I pick up the pillow. I pull the sheets taut. I make the bed. She was here just last night. Sleeping in this bed. Evan is beside me now.

"We'll find her," he says.

It's a trope, I tell him. It's a cliché. Girls always disappear. They make themselves small, and then they disappear.

"And if they don't disappear, they go insane. That's it. Those are the only two options we get."

"I thought the cliché was that girls were always in pursuit of boys," Evan says.

"So we have three options!" I yell.

That I am mad at him is inexplicable, incomprehensible. This isn't his fault. No more than it is my fault. And yet, I think, if only he had been less cavalier about the whole thing, had been more concerned about the walk to the grocery store, her coy voice on the phone.

His hands are on my shoulders. His fingers are pushing at the muscles, only he's missing the muscle and hitting the bone, and I shrug off his hands and walk away, down the hall, into the kitchen, where the dishes have been washed and are sitting neatly in the drying rack. He is behind me.

"She knew," I say. "Last night when we went for pizza, and she ate pie with us, and she cleared our plates, and she washed them. She had already planned to leave. I know it."

"She knew the second she arrived, Val."

I don't want this to be true. I don't want to believe it.

Evan is going to retrace our steps.

"From the last three weeks?" I ask. "All of them?"

"You stay," he says, kissing me on the forehead. "In case she comes back."

My brother calls again. He asks for our address. He wants to know how he is supposed to get from the airport to our house, which is an hour and a half away.

"Rent a car," I say.

And because I know what he is thinking, I tell him we'll pay for it.

———

Evan and I sit on the porch. We wait. This is what you do on the first day while you wait for a teenager to return, which they usually do, almost always do.

You check the local newspaper headlines.

You drive around the neighborhood.

You turn on the TV in the middle of the day, expecting to see her face, her body.

You try to distract yourself with small tasks.

You create false deadlines. She will be back by noon. And when she doesn't arrive, it's by three. Then dinner becomes your arbitrary marker, and you push dinner later and later until your husband puts a burger and fries in front of you.

You feel you shouldn't eat it.

You feel you don't deserve it.

But you eat it because you haven't eaten all day and you are hungry.

---

I watch my brother, a short, balding man with a beard, get out of the car. He looks different. Older and tired and more like our father than I have ever noticed.

I expect the trunk to pop open, for him to pull out his suitcase, but instead I see my brother swing a backpack over one shoulder as he walks to where I am standing at the front door. And now I am crying. Because all he's brought is a backpack. Because it's been three years since I've seen him. Because his daughter is missing. Because it's his first time on an airplane, for this. Because he warned me, and I didn't believe him.

He wraps his arms around me, and I feel like I don't deserve this either. His comfort. But I take it. It has always been this way with us. Fierce on the phone. Quick with blame. All of that gone when we see each other.

That night, we all pretend to sleep, and in the morning, while I'm still in bed, covers pulled up around my face, eyes closed because I am tired, I hear Evan in the bathroom. He is showering. Shaving. I hear the toothbrush against the sink. And then he is standing at the closet. He is dressing. I sit up in bed.

"You can't," I say, but I know as soon as I say it that he will. He has to. If he calls in sick again he will lose his job.

———

The police station is empty. Just a small waiting room with three seats. An officer sits behind a desk. I hope my brother is comforted by how quiet it is in here. I hope he feels, as I do, that this nice man behind the counter is going to help us. I tell him that my brother has just arrived, that my niece hasn't been seen in over thirty-six hours, and that we need to talk with Officer Peterson.

"She's not on duty," he says. "You'll have to talk with me." My brother stands with his hands in his pockets. As he talks with this new officer, I listen.

Yes, she has done this before, many times, about a year ago it started. Every few months. Out all night. Gone for days at a time. Once much longer—more than a week. That was during winter break.

I look at him. What he is saying—none of it makes sense. It's not the same girl, I want to say.

After we leave the police station, we stop for coffee, and when we get back in the car, I make the absurd offer to give him a tour of town. Maybe a drive out to the beach. He has never seen the Pacific Ocean.

"I told you. You couldn't take your eyes off her. I told you. You can't leave her alone."

"We were sleeping," I say.

"Before that? All those other days?"

I lie: "We never left her side."

We go home and sit on the stoop outside the house, waiting. I ask him about his job, and he says what he always says: it's a paycheck. He asks me about mine, and I go on for too long and in too much detail about how we think mantis shrimp have a different kind of color vision, how we're trying to get a reading from photoreceptor cells but can't even fit a recording device onto them because they're so small. When I look at him, I can see I've lost him.

"She wants to come live here next year," I say. "After she graduates, if she decides to take a gap year."

"Is that what she told you?" he says.

I nod. I'm trying to gauge whether he is hurt or angry or relieved, but he just shakes his head. He laughs a little.

"She doesn't have enough credits to graduate next year," he says. "She's still considered a sophomore."

We sit for a long time, watching cars drive by the house. Across the street two dogs bark at the fence. The owner comes out. Tells them to get inside, to cut it out. A kid rides by on a bike. Another one follows on a skateboard. They are singing a song that is popular this summer, one that is played over and over on the radio.

Evan comes home at 5:15. He doesn't say it, but I can tell he has had a bad day. He kisses me and pats my brother on the shoulder.

"Anything?" Evan asks.

"Nothing," he says.

That evening, the police call. They ask us to come down to the station. They have a few more questions. They have something we should see.

We are in the car and down the road before anyone speaks.

"Did he say what it is?" Evan asks. "What they want to show us?"

"A picture of some kind," my brother says. "They wouldn't tell me more than that."

*A picture*, I think. Of Didi alone? At the airport, boarding a plane? Getting into a strange car? Her body, my god. Would they ask us to come down to identify a picture of her body? Would they be so casual about it on the phone?

I hope, when we walk through the police station doors, that Officer Peterson will be there to greet us. She's not. It's a different officer. Someone we've never talked to before, and it's my brother he needs to speak to. They disappear down the hall, and Evan and I sit on chairs in the waiting room. I reach for his hand.

"Was your day okay?" I ask.

He turns to me. I think he will tell me about the apple trees he pruned incorrectly or how he overfertilized an entire shipment of succulents. I'm expecting news of broken terra-cotta pots or bamboo sticks that never arrived.

"When you left," he says, "this is what it felt like. Exactly like this."

The officer behind the bulletproof window stretches, arms overhead, and yawns. It takes me longer than it should to realize we aren't talking about Evan's day, or the plants he tended to, or the nursery at all.

I shake my head. "You knew where I was going," I say. "You could have called me. You could have come to visit whenever you wanted."

"I'm not talking about college, Val. I'm talking about all those other times you disappeared, before you left for college—those nights you didn't call, the weekends you just vanished. And later, all those research trips, how you extended them again and again, sometimes without even telling me, sometimes for weeks at a time."

We have had this conversation before. More than once. Dozens of times. But I see something new in his face now, not a bitterness but a sadness, and I am convinced this is the first step to him leaving me—maybe for a year, maybe longer. Before I can say anything to talk him out of it, my brother is coming back down the hall, the officer behind him.

My brother shakes his head. "Wasn't her," he says, and I can see he is near tears, shocked by what he has been forced to look at.

———

It all ends just as Officer Peterson promised.

We drive back to the house from the police station, and she is there. My brother is out of the car before I even come to a full stop. I sit in the driver's seat while he goes to her. Evan doesn't move. He sits beside me. We watch.

I wonder how many times this scene has played out. How many times has a girl returned to find no one is waiting for her?

And what is it you want to know? Whether my

brother hits her? (He doesn't.) Whether she is crying? (She isn't.) Or do you want to know where she was, what she was doing? (She will refuse to say.) Is she harmed? (Not in any way that I can tell. No scrapes or bruises. No broken bones. No blood.)

Because you are wondering. Because people always wonder. Because under these circumstances, it matters what she is wearing, by which I mean it matters to me:

My clothes. A pair of jeans—black and tight and cropped. A white T-shirt, baggy and see-through, a baby-blue tank top underneath. Black summer sandals. Beige stitching at the seams. Thin leather straps that loop around her heels, hug her toes, and, I am certain, have left her blistered. I leave Evan in the car, and I go to her. I pull her to me. I feel her body against mine, rigid and small and hard. Her heart pounds against my palm. I fold her in. I tuck her in as close as I can and hold her for as long as she lets me. When she begins to pull away, I let go, certain there is nothing I can say, nothing I can do, to make her stay. So I do the only thing I can. I pull her hands out of her pockets. I push her shoulders back. I am not gentle.

# NOTES

In the nine years I worked on this collection of stories, I consulted many sources. It would be impossible to list each one here, but a few stand out in their influence, and I would like to acknowledge my debt to them and thank the authors. Studs Terkel's *Working* first sparked my interest in labor and the stories we tell about it. On matters of mushing and mushers, I'm indebted to *Dog Driver: A Guide for the Serious Musher* by Miki Collins and Julie Collins, and *Race Across Alaska: First Woman to Win the Iditarod Tells Her Story* by Libby Riddles and Tim Jones. *Building With Stone* by Charles McRaven and *Stone Work: Reflections on Serious Play and Other Aspects of Country Life* by John Jerome were both helpful in understanding the materials and techniques of stonemasonry. Robert Macfarlane's *Underland: A Deep Time Journey* was crucial in my understanding of underground rivers, and *Home Ground: A Guide to the American Landscape*, edited by Barry Lopez and Debra Gwartney, proved an invaluable—and gorgeous—reference. The *CRM Archeology Podcast* kept me company on many long drives and introduced me to the labor of archeology and the realities of that work, and the National Register of Historic Places was an important resource on issues of preservation. On matters of search and rescue, thanks to the National Park Service blog "Search and Rescue: Lessons from the Field," as well as Robert J. Koester's manual *Lost Person Behavior: A Search and Rescue Guide on Where to Look for Land, Air, and Water,* from which I've drawn the concept of "bending the map." On matters of mantis shrimp, I am especially grateful to Dr. Kate Feller for the tour of her lab at the University of Cambridge. Finally, thanks to Cornell Lab, Audubon, and the Royal Society for the Protection of Birds for the reports on the rise of wildlife trafficking and the threat it poses to the birds. I have tried my best to get the facts right; I have, at times, taken liberties with the details in service of the stories.

# ACKNOWLEDGMENTS

Thanks to Ariana Kelly, Julie Stern, April Darcy, Kate McQuade, and Jennifer Sinor for reading everything, multiple times, and offering such wise advice when I could no longer see what was at the heart of this book. Other friends and colleagues provided invaluable feedback, generous encouragement, and the occasional fact checking along the way: Kiran Puri, Daryln Brewer Hoffstot, Katya Apekina, David Pugh, Jennifer Solheim, Charles Waugh, Ben Gunsberg, Michael Sowder, Rowena Leong Singer, Liz Melchor, Kevin Fitton, Dan McDermott, Ryan Wilson, Adam Rose, Zachary Green Asher, Kate Feller, Andrew May, and Suzette Bruggeman.

Special thanks to the Bennington Writing Seminars, especially Joan Wickersham, Amy Hempel, Jill McCorkle, Megan Mayhew Bergman, Paul Yoon, and Bret Anthony Johnston. Your ongoing support at crucial moments of this book's long journey kept me moving forward.

Thanks are due to the editors who published earlier versions of these stories in their journals and anthologies: Jennifer Cranfill and Greg Brownderville at *Southwest Review* ("The Handler"), Wendy Lesser and Rose Whitmore at *Threepenny Review* ("The Stonemason's Wife"), Sven Birkerts and William Pierce at *AGNI* ("Bending the Map"), Katrina Turner and Benjamin Anastas at *Bennington Review* ("Call Up the Waters"),

Michael Nye at *Story* ("What the Birds Knew"), Emily Smith Gilbert at *Southampton Review* ("Shovelbums"), Cody Lee at *Greensboro Review* ("Fixed Blade"), and Yuka Igarashi at Catapult ("The Handler," in *PEN America Best Debut Stories 2017*).

PEN America and the Robert J. Dau Foundation offered early recognition of my first published story; thank you, Fernanda Dau Fisher, for making it possible. I am also grateful to the Elizabeth George Foundation and the Barbara Deming Memorial Fund for providing early financial support as I drafted the first stories of this manuscript, and to Writing By Writers and the Brush Creek Foundation of the Arts for providing the gifts of time and space to draft the final stories.

Joey McGarvey, my fabulous editor, thank you for your enthusiastic support of this book and for bringing such wisdom and generosity to the editing process. Other champions at Milkweed: Bailey Hutchinson, Daniel Slager, Mary Austin Speaker, Yanna Demkiewicz, Morgan Larocca, Shannon Blackmer, and Jordan Koluch. May every writer have such an amazing team ushering her first book into the world.

To my family—Karen, Ed, Tracey, Tod, Shawn, and Nate—for the unflagging love, support, and laughter. To Anitra, Dave, Phil, Andy, and Emily for welcoming me so fully into your family and for celebrating all things big and small. And to Seth—for believing in me and this book, and for cutting all the right words from each of these stories.

*Andrew McAllister*

Amber Caron's work has appeared in *PEN America Best Debut Short Stories, AGNI, Threepenny Review, Story, Bennington Review, Southwest Review, Longreads, The Writer's Chronicle*, and elsewhere. She is the recipient of the PEN/Robert J. Dau Short Story Prize for Emerging Writers, *Southwest Review*'s McGinnis-Ritchie Award for fiction, and grants from the Elizabeth George Foundation and the Barbara Deming Memorial Fund. She lives in Logan, Utah, where she is an assistant professor of English at Utah State University and an assistant fiction editor at *AGNI*.

milkweed
EDITIONS

Founded as a nonprofit organization in 1980, Milkweed Editions is an independent publisher. Our mission is to identify, nurture, and publish transformative literature, and build an engaged community around it.

Milkweed Editions is based in Bdé Óta Othúŋwe (Minneapolis) within Mní Sota Makhóčhe, the traditional homeland of the Dakhóta people. Residing here since time immemorial, Dakhóta people still call Mní Sota Makhóčhe home, with four federally recognized Dakhóta nations and many more Dakhóta people residing in what is now the state of Minnesota. Due to continued legacies of colonization, genocide, and forced removal, generations of Dakhóta people remain disenfranchised from their traditional homeland. Presently, Mní Sota Makhóčhe has become a refuge and home for many Indigenous nations and peoples, including seven federally recognized Ojibwe nations. We humbly encourage our readers to reflect upon the historical legacies held in the lands they occupy.

milkweed.org

Milkweed Editions, an independent nonprofit publisher, gratefully acknowledges sustaining support from our Board of Directors; the Alan B. Slifka Foundation and its president, Riva Ariella Ritvo-Slifka; the Amazon Literary Partnership; the Ballard Spahr Foundation; *Copper Nickel*; the McKnight Foundation; the National Endowment for the Arts; the National Poetry Series; and other generous contributions from foundations, corporations, and individuals. Also, this activity is made possible by the voters of Minnesota through a Minnesota State Arts Board Operating Support grant, thanks to a legislative appropriation from the arts and cultural heritage fund. For a full listing of Milkweed Editions supporters, please visit milkweed.org.

Interior design by Tijqua Daiker
Typeset in Caslon


Adobe Caslon Pro was created by Carol Twombly
for Adobe Systems in 1990. Her design was inspired by
the family of typefaces cut by the celebrated engraver
William Caslon I, whose family foundry served
England with clean, elegant type from the early
Enlightenment through the turn of the
twentieth century.